RUSE

**A murder and a series of heists test
Police Scotland**

PETE BRASSETT

THE
BOOK
FOLKS

Paperback published by The Book Folks

London, 2022

ISBN 978-1-913516-20-8

www.thebookfolks.com

RUSE is the thirteenth novel by Pete Brassett to feature detectives Munro and West. Details about the other books can be found at the end of this one. All of these books can be enjoyed on their own, or as a series.

For Bridie.
Wife, mother, friend, and fusspot.

*"Courage isn't having the strength to go on,
it's going on when you don't have the strength."*

Napoleon Bonaparte

Prologue

With a mop of grey hair, a goatee beard, and a guitar slung across his back, the pony-tailed Tam McDonnell – a slender sixty-five-year-old with a penchant for roll-ups and Bourbon – could have been mistaken for one of Nashville's touring elite as he hopped into a camper van, slipped an unlit cigarette between his lips, and left the bustling dockside of Leith for the comparatively sedate streets of Ayr.

As co-founder of the Gallus Advertising Agency and the creative genius behind ground-breaking campaigns for the *Glasgow Metro*, Scottish spring water, a high street bank, and a mobile phone company, McDonnell had enjoyed more than his fair share of success but after forty years of wining and dining clients and a liver fast approaching its use-by date, he realised his days were numbered, not least because a new breed of politically correct creatives, who were about as cutting edge as a butter knife, were snapping at his heels.

Faced with trying to salvage what was left of a dwindling career or making the most of a God-given opportunity to follow his dreams, he opted for the latter, accepted a cash offer for his share of the business, and set his sights on opening a laid-back bar with live performances from some of Scotland's finest folk singers.

However, six months down the line, a disillusioned McDonnell, having sunk his severance into the refurbishment of a run-down pub on Alloway Street, was left wondering why The Bonnie Selkie was failing to attract the customers he so desperately needed.

Loitering in the doorway, he pulled a Zippo from the pocket of his denim jacket and lit a cigarette, oblivious to the gaze of a curious young man watching intently from across the street.

Bemused by the sight of a poor man's Willie Nelson drawing forlornly on a roll-up, Jonnie Miller – full-time DJ, illegal rave organiser, and supplier of poppers, puff, and paste to his loyal followers – pushed his straw hat to the back of his head and folded his arms as he contemplated the hand-painted image of a buxom mermaid swinging above the door.

With zero qualifications and an aversion to any conventional form of employment, the cash-conscious twenty-eight-year-old, as wily as a market trader, was blessed with an uncanny knack for sniffing out money-making opportunities like a pig snuffling for truffles.

'Alright, pal?' he said, as he swaggered across the street. 'When's the funeral?'

McDonnell glanced across and smiled.

'The way things are,' he said, 'it could be tomorrow.'

'How so?'

'I've a bar stocked with quality booze, my happy hour runs from 11am to 9pm, and I've some decent acts playing on the weekends but no-one's coming through the door.'

'Sounds bad,' said Miller. 'What kind of acts do you have? Is it comedy?'

'No, no. Top-class country and folk.'

Miller shoved his hands in his pockets, looked to the ground, and tried not to laugh.

'I take it you're not a fan,' said McDonnell.

'Don't get me wrong. I mean, there's nothing wrong with a wee bit of Johnny Cash now and then but generally speaking I prefer my music a bit more *upbeat*.'

'Each to his own.'

'I'm curious,' said Miller, 'why here? I mean, there's not many cowboys in Ayrshire.'

'Because,' said McDonnell, 'I was born here, and for what it's worth, I've done my research. There's plenty of country gigs over at the town hall and the theatre.'

'Right enough, but have you seen the folk who go there? They're not exactly minted, and they're not going to spend money on drink when they've already forked out for a ticket.'

'Is that so?'

'Aye! Maybe you should've picked somewhere a bit more lively.'

'I'm done with lively,' said McDonnell. 'I'm wanting to take things easy now.'

'Fair enough. So, what's your plan?'

McDonnell flicked his head to an A4 sheet of paper taped inside the window.

'*Help Wanted*,' said Miller. 'Just what kind of help is it you're after?'

'The psychological kind, I think.'

'I can do that.'

'Can you indeed?' said McDonnell. 'And what makes you an expert?'

Miller leaned forward and spoke as if divulging a secret.

'I can get inside people's heads,' he said, softly. 'I know what folk want, and I know how to give it to them.'

'I used to think that too, but as far as running a pub's concerned, I think I'm out of my depth. Do you have name?'

'Jonnie.'

'So, tell me, Jonnie. What is it you do exactly?'

'Anything. Anything for cash, as long as it doesn't involve reading, writing, or lifting.'

Miller stepped to one side, poked his head through the door, and nodded approvingly as he surveyed the plethora of framed photographs and vintage Americana adorning the walls.

'Very nice,' he said. 'Classy. It looks classy.'

'You mean expensive?'

'No, no. I mean tasteful. You've done a cracking job, I'll give you that.'

'Thanks very much but compliments won't pay the bills. What I need is folk at the bar.'

'Then I'm your man.'

'Right, let's have it,' said McDonnell. 'You tell me why I should hire you.'

'Because I can run a bar,' said Miller, 'I can spin a turntable, and I know enough folk to have this place hoachin with drinkers on a Saturday night.'

'And what's it going to cost?'

Miller pursed his lips and frowned as he pondered an offer.

'Right,' he said, 'you've not got money to burn, that's obvious, and I need to prove myself to you, so I'll cut you a deal.'

'Here we go.'

'I'll do you a Saturday night for free.'

'Tomorrow?'

'Aye.'

'For free?'

'Aye! No fee, just twenty percent of the takings. If you're happy with the footfall then maybe we can come to a more permanent arrangement.'

McDonnell took a puff of his cigarette, blew the smoke skywards, and stared at Miller.

'Alright,' he said. 'You're on. I mean, what have I got to lose?'

'Nothing,' said Miller with a wink, 'but you've everything to gain. One thing though, if we're going to make this work, you'll have to put your dreams on hold for a week or two.'

'Sorry,' said McDonnell, 'I'm not with you.'

'Folk here,' said Miller, 'the younger folk, they're not into country music so we have to educate them first, but to do that we need to get them through the door, and to get them through the door, you're going to have to make some sacrifices.'

'Like what?'

'TV. No TV means no football, and no football means no punters.'

'What else?'

'Cancel your gigs, just for a wee while. Like I say, folk like me, we're not into songs about divorce, or pick-up trucks, or dead dogs, we're into *happy*.'

'So you're saying I should turn this place into just another pub?'

'Only for a wee while. I'll start mixing in some country tunes in a week or two but by then they'll be hooked on the place.'

'Well, I'm not convinced,' said McDonnell, 'but we'll give it a go. Right, give me your number and tell me what you need.'

'Just the telly. I'll drop by tomorrow to set up and by eight o'clock they'll be queuing round the block.'

* * *

As a former creative whose erratic working hours revolved around sporadic bouts of inspiration and booze-laden lunches with marketing executives keen to discuss the progress of their latest campaign over a four course lunch rather than the telephone, Tam McDonnell was not in the least bit perturbed by Jonnie Miller's tardiness, however, by 4:17pm with his phone going straight to voicemail, he resigned himself to the fact that he'd been duped by an opportunist young enough to be his grandson when, drawn by the sound of a rasping exhaust, he ventured outside and winced as a bleary-eyed Miller tumbled out of a dark blue Subaru.

'I'd just about given up,' he said.

'You know your problem?' said Miller, with a smirk. 'No faith. I may be late but some things are worth waiting for.'

'I'll reserve judgement on that. Heavy night?'

'Nothing a wee bridie and a couple of Red Bulls can't fix. Now, I need to get a wiggle on.'

'Will I give you a hand?' said McDonnell. 'With your records and turntables and that?'

Miller laughed as he reached into the car.

'Keep up, Granda,' he said, waving a laptop. 'There's no turntables, it's all on this! Right, stick the telly on, they'll be here soon.'

He dashed inside, swung a table onto the small stage and wired up his MacBook as McDonnell fumbled with the remote control.

'I'm not one for football,' he said, 'which channel is it you're wanting?'

'BBC Scot. It's Hearts v Rangers so it might get a bit lively in here.'

'I'd rather boil my head.'

'Feel free,' said Miller, 'but do it somewhere else. I'll see you back here around eleven.'

'Oh, no,' said McDonnell, bluntly. 'No offence, son, but I don't know you from Adam and I'm not about to leave my pub in the hands of a total stranger. Besides, you'll be needing me to serve the customers.'

'I will not. I'll have Freya with me. When it comes to pulling pints, she's poetry in motion.'

'And just how much am I paying to have the goddess of love behind the bar?'

'Hee-haw. She's a part of the deal.'

'Well, I'm still not leaving,' said McDonnell. 'I'll be in the corner where I can keep an eye on things.'

* * *

Assuming that fifty percent of the tanked-up football fanatics about to grace his pub would be supporters of the losing side who'd vent their angst by instigating a mass brawl resulting in several broken noses and a visit from Police Scotland, McDonnell helped himself to a large Jack Daniel's and settled anxiously into a corner seat, his curiosity roused by a gaggle of trendy twenty-somethings filing through the door swiftly followed by a slim brunette who winked at Miller, tossed her bag behind the bar, and familiarised herself with the till before facing the line of thirsty punters.

'Right,' she said, with an impish grin. 'Who's first?'

Captivated by the charm of the sassy and clearly confident young woman, McDonnell stood, took a large sip of whisky, and watched in awe as a spritely Freya Thomson pirouetted behind the bar taking orders, pouring pints, and serving shots, with the fluid dexterity of a Bolshoi ballerina as the pub quickly filled to breaking point.

Save for a fleeting moment when the sound of breaking glass threatened to induce an overdue heart attack, McDonnell – conceding that, in light of the excitable but otherwise well-behaved crowd, the pub was in safe hands – heaved a sigh of relief as the referee blew full time, and slipped away to enjoy a lengthy and altogether much quieter spot of supper at the Meridian café before returning some three and a half hours later to find a handful of jaded revellers milling about on the street, laughing as they drained the dregs from their glasses.

'If I'm honest,' he said as he entered the empty pub, 'I was expecting carnage. Have you called time?'

Miller smiled as he took a swig of bottled water.

'Aye, of course! And if you look around, you'll see your bar's still intact.'

'Just as well. Where's your pal, Freya?'

'Long gone,' said Miller, 'she's pure shattered and I'm not surprised, she's been working like a dog.'

'So it went alright? No bother?'

'No bother at all. Apart from some ned who fancied his chances with Freya, but she soon told him where to go. Other than that, we had a cracking night. I even got some Tammy Wynette on for you.'

'Tammy Wynette? Are you joking me?'

'Aye! Well, it was the track she did with The KLF but it's the same thing really.'

'Right,' said McDonnell, 'I'd best clear up. You should take yourself off, no offence, but you look like you need the rest.'

'Aye, right enough.'

'But before you go, let's see how we did, shall we?'

McDonnell strolled behind the bar, pressed "shift report" on the touch screen, and groaned.

'What's up?' said Miller.

'Technology!' said McDonnell, rolling his eyes. 'This till's clearly up the spout!'

'How so?'

'It's saying the day's takings are two thousand, nine hundred, and eighty-eight pounds!'

'And you think that's a problem?'

'Aye! Of course it is! Two hundred would be nearer the mark!'

'I'd open the till if I were you.'

McDonnell drew a short sharp breath as the drawer slid open and turned to face Miller with a look of bewilderment on his face.

'Are you joking me?' he said, softly. 'So, three grand, that's the correct amount?'

'I'd say it's spot on.'

'You've taken more money in one night than I have in...'

'Happy to oblige,' said Miller with a smile. 'Like I said, I know what people want and I know how to give it to them. So, how's your maths?'

'Dodgy at best.'

'Then I'll help you out. Twenty percent of three grand is six hundred quid. Roughly speaking.'

'And you've earned every penny,' said McDonnell as he counted out the cash. 'I don't know how to thank you, son. Really, I don't.'

'Six hundred's thanks enough. So, are you wanting me back?'

'Are you mad? Aye! Of course.'

'Suits me.'

'Hold on, will we do the Friday as well?'

'No, no, that'd be overkill,' said Miller. 'I'll catch you next week.'

* * *

Dumbfounded by the day's takings McDonnell bolted the doors, helped himself to a celebratory drink and, taking a moment to reflect, raised a glass to the young Jonnie Miller before clearing the tables and heading for the lavatories with a mop and bucket under his arm.

Accepting the occasional blocked toilet as an unfortunate consequence of running any pub or club, he dismissed the "out of order" sign taped outside the ladies, stepped inside, and blenched at the stench of vomit seeping from beneath a cubicle door.

Had the pool of puke been all he'd had to contend with, it would have been nothing more than a slightly unpleasant end to an otherwise perfect day, however, the sight of a blood-soaked Freya Thomson slumped on the bowl with a waiter's corkscrew protruding from her neck had him dashing to the gents.

Chapter 1

With a face full of stubble, filthy jeans, and a battered, leather car coat, the maverick DS Duncan Reid – who believed rules were for bending, lines were for crossing, and locks were for picking – enjoyed a questionable reputation for going undetected amongst the drug-addled jakeys of the county in his quest to snare the rising number of pushers and dealers blighting his patch. However, when dealing with crimes of another nature, his dishevelled appearance had many a suspect questioning the authenticity of his badge.

'Sorry,' said McDonnell, his hands trembling as he sipped his whisky, 'no offence but you look like the kind of fella who could have done it.'

'None taken,' said Duncan as he ruffled his unkempt hair. 'Now, there's no rush, take as long as you like. So, you were heading for the toilets?'

'Aye. As I say, if it was just the pile of sick or a blocked pan, I could have coped, but to find her lying there like that, dear God, that's not something I want to see again in a hurry.'

'How long had you known her?'

'I didn't. I never even got to speak to her. She was Jonnie's pal, he'd arranged tonight's event.'

'This Jonnie, does he have a surname?'

'Aye, Miller. Jonnie Miller. I have his number if you want it.'

'Not necessary,' said Duncan, 'we've got it too. He's a familiar face down the station.'

'So he's a criminal?'

'Not really. He's a talented kid, just not very good at organising the paperwork when it comes to arranging his parties.'

'Well, that's a relief,' said McDonnell. 'You had me worried for a moment.'

'So what made you take him on?'

'It was pure chance. I was out front doing nothing in particular when he came by. He asked why I was looking so glum.'

'And why were you?'

'This place,' said McDonnell, shaking his head, 'the business. It's not been working, not the way I'd planned. I was on the verge of shutting up shop until last night.'

'Go on.'

'I explained my dilemma. I said I needed folk coming through the door so he said he'd organise a gig for me. He all but guaranteed to have the place packed to the rafters.'

'And was it?'

'Aye, like nothing I've seen,' said McDonnell. 'He just about saved my bacon.'

'And the girl?'

'Freya's her name.'

Duncan raised his eyebrows prompting McDonnell to continue.

'That's it,' he said, shrugging his shoulders. 'I don't have a second name.'

'So when exactly was the last time you saw her?'

'When I left for my supper, it would have been around eight or eight-thirty, not that I could actually see her, like I say, the place was packed.'

'And when you came back?'

'It was after eleven. She was gone. Jonnie was packing up his gear, and there were folk on the pavement outside.'

'Did Jonnie see her leave?'

'I assumed so,' said McDonnell. 'I asked where she was so I could thank her but he simply said she'd left.'

'And what happened next?'

McDonnell leaned back in his seat, looked to the ceiling, and frowned.

'We had a chat,' he said. 'Nothing major. I asked him how it went, if there was any trouble. He said there was one broken glass, but that was just an accident behind the bar. Some fella fancied his chances with Freya and ended up with a bruised ego, and we ran out of Jägermeister – that was it. Then I checked the takings and that was something of a revelation. More money went into that till in one night than I've taken in months, so I gave him his cut and–'

'Ho! Slow down,' said Duncan. 'His cut?'

'Aye. I couldn't afford to pay him anything so we had a deal. Twenty percent of the takings.'

'Very generous.'

'It was money well spent. I was hoping he'd be back next week but after this…'

'Don't worry,' said Duncan, 'if all goes to plan we'll be out of your hair in a few days. There's no reason why you'll not be open for the weekend. Now, next question, was there anything you noticed about Freya, anything unusual? Was she nervous, maybe? Fidgety? On edge?'

'No, no. Quite the opposite. She came through that door with her head held high, put her bag behind the bar, and worked her magic.'

'Hold on,' said Duncan, raising his hand. 'Her bag?'

'Aye. A wee thing.'

'Can you describe it?'

'Green, I think. Olive green. Not too big, about the size of a paperback. She'd been wearing it around her neck.'

'And is it where she left it?'

'I've not looked. I thought if she'd left, she'd have taken it with her.'

Duncan stood and backed away from the room to check with the SOCO in the lavatory before returning empty-handed and rummaging amongst the racks of empty glasses, the boxes of crisps, and the bin of empty bottles beneath the bar.

'Well, it's not here,' he said, returning to his seat. 'Looks like someone's had it away.'

'So you think she was mugged?' said McDonnell. 'Was it some chancer after her purse?'

'Maybe. You've no cameras here, have you?'

'None. I tell a lie, there's one. It's directly above the till.'

'No worries,' said Duncan. 'I'll be having a chat with Miller soon enough, we'll try and trace everyone who came to your gig, chances are someone would have seen him leave with it.'

'Maybe not,' said McDonnell. 'Not if he left by the back.'

'The back?'

'Aye, the fire door was open.'

'And where does that lead? Is it a yard, or an alleyway?'

'No, no. The car park,' said McDonnell. 'It runs between here and Dalblair Road.'

Duncan rolled his eyes, stood, and reached for his phone.

'Wait here,' he said as he headed outside. 'I'll be two minutes.'

* * *

Wondering if he'd said too much or not enough, McDonnell left his seat, helped himself to another shot of

JD, and knocked it back with the pained expression of someone taking a dose of castor oil.

'Right,' said Duncan, as he breezed through the door. 'We're going to cordon off the rear of the building too and we'll have some extra officers combing the car park so you'll not be able go out the back. In fact, Mr McDonnell, you'll not be able to stay here at all.'

'Where will I go?'

'No need to worry. Pack yourself a bag and I'll get someone to run you to a hotel for a couple of nights. The Mercure's just around the corner, we'll pop you in there. Are you okay with that?'

'Aye, of course. No bother.'

'Good. I'll need to get a full statement off you in the morning so I'll send someone to pick you up around nine. Now, my advice to you is to get some sleep.'

* * *

Had she worked for the local council, Kay Grogan – an elfin scenes of crime officer with an insatiable appetite for cataloguing the gory aftermath of any stabbing, shooting, or suicide – might have awarded The Bonnie Selkie a resounding pass on the hygiene certificate were it not for the pungent puddle of puke in the ladies' washroom which, whilst not uncommon after a raucous night on the tiles, was made all the more intriguing by the presence of a young girl slumped on a nearby toilet bowl.

Keen to capture the contorted features of her latest subject, she hovered impatiently by the door until forensic pathologist Andy McLeod had completed a cursory examination of the body before snapping away with the unbridled enthusiasm of a paparazzo at a film festival.

'That's a belter!' she said, grinning as she craned her neck for a close-up. 'I've not seen one like this before!'

McLeod, deeming the SOCO a welcome if not slightly unhinged breath of fresh air when compared to the handful of dour, silent types he often had to work with, took a step back and lowered his mask.

'Sometimes,' he said, 'you give me the fear.'

'How so?'

'Because you've more in common with Vlad the Impaler than Mary Poppins.'

'Flattery will get you nowhere.'

'How long before I can get her bagged and tagged?'

'Give me twenty,' said Grogan, 'and she's all yours. Anything else?'

'Aye. If it's not too much trouble, I'll have a bag of the vomitus to go.'

'You should lay off the takeaways,' said Duncan as he sauntered up behind him, 'they're not as healthy as you think. So, what's the story?'

McLeod turned to Duncan and smiled.

'Well, I'm not one to speculate but I've a feeling she may have been stabbed in the neck.'

'Nothing wrong with your eyesight. Go on.'

'The perp scored a bullseye on the jugular, that's why the cubicle's such a fetching shade of red.'

'So you think he knew what he was doing?'

'That's anyone's guess,' said McLeod, 'maybe he did, or maybe it was just a lucky strike.'

Duncan leaned against the door and scratched his chin as he pondered the attack.

'Either way,' he said, 'if she was spouting like a fountain, would the perp have been in the line of fire?'

'Undoubtedly.'

'Not necessarily,' said Grogan, 'not if she was attacked from behind.'

'Nice theory,' said McLeod, 'but going by the angle of entry, I'd say that was highly unlikely.'

'So,' said Duncan, 'if she was facing her attacker, I suppose there's the possibility that she may have known him.'

'Aye. Or her. After all, we are in the ladies. She also has contusions to the neck and the wrists. The likelihood is that's where she was held while she was grappling with her assailant. She put up a struggle, that's for sure.'

'If that was me,' said Grogan, 'I'd have screamed the house down.'

'She probably did,' said Duncan, 'but with the racket that was going on out there I doubt anyone would have heard her.'

'I've some good news, too,' said McLeod. 'There's a couple of hairs and some blood beneath the fingernails of her right hand.'

'How is that good?'

'Because there's none on her fingers or her palm, which means it didn't get there because she was clutching her own throat. I'd say she scratched her attacker so whoever did this will almost certainly have some grazing to the head and possibly some lacerations to the face or neck.'

'Good for her,' said Duncan, 'that'll make our job a wee bit easier, I'm sure.'

'Just a thought,' said McLeod, 'it's a Saturday night, we're in a pub, and the fella would have been covered in blood. Did nobody see him leave?'

'We don't know yet but maybe not. The back door was open. It's looking like he might have legged it across the car park to Dalblair Road.'

'Well, it's busy enough down there. I'm sure you'll have a fair few witnesses to call upon.'

'Aye,' said Duncan, 'if they decide to come forward. So, back to Freya, how long?'

'Not long at all,' said McLeod. 'A couple of hours, three, tops.'

Duncan pulled up his sleeve and glanced at his watch.

'So, anytime between 10pm and now?'

'Aye, thereabouts.'

'And she bled to death?'

Well, that would be the obvious assumption,' said McLeod. 'With a wound to the jugular it wouldn't take much more than five minutes to bleed out but, at the risk of sounding pedantic, there's a chance the sheer shock of her ordeal could have induced a heart attack, it all depends on how healthy she was. And then there's the vomit.'

'What about it?'

'I'm not convinced it's hers.'

'How so?'

'There's not a trace of it on her face, in her mouth, or in the nose.'

'Could she not have puked then cleaned herself up before she was attacked?'

'I suppose it's possible,' said McLeod, 'but then you have to ask yourself the question, what made her throw up in the first place?'

'I am.'

'And?'

'Well, she's a bonnie wee lass,' said Duncan, 'I'm thinking someone could've spiked her drink.'

'No,' said McLeod flatly. 'For two reasons. One, she'd have to have a stomach so sensitive, she'd not even be able to eat, and two, I can guarantee that if her drink was spiked, she'd have passed out before she had a chance to retch.'

'That's told me, then.'

'Do you know who she is?'

'Her name's Freya,' said Duncan, 'and so far, that's all we know. Does she not have anything in her pockets, a bank card maybe?'

'Nothing, but surely the owner would know who she is. Does he not have her details?'

'No. She was casual, drafted in for just the one night.'

'Poor thing,' said Grogan, as she left the cubicle. 'Sounds like a classic case of wrong time, wrong place. Right, she's all yours.'

'Thank you very much,' said McLeod. 'Before I zip her up, how's your man?'

'The owner?' said Duncan. 'Aye, he's okay, a bit shaken up, as you'd expect. To be honest, the poor fella's worried about losing his licence, he's had a rough time of it recently.'

'In what way?'

'This place. It's not been doing well. Last night was the first good night he's had in months.'

'And probably the last.'

'No, no. I told him if we're done on time, then there's no reason why he couldn't open by the weekend. He'll probably have another cracking night with folk queuing up to see where a young lassie was murdered.'

'Aye, and if young Kay wasn't a SOCO, she'd be the first in line.'

'Right enough,' said Grogan. 'Now, you two, clear off, I've got stacks to do before I even get outside. Duncan, are you heading back to the office?'

'Aye, but there's someone I have to see first.'

'No bother. I'll drop by when I'm done.'

Chapter 2

Were Jonnie Miller to surrender the lease on his rented flat in the loft space of a four-storey tenement on Smith Street, the brochure would probably describe the converted garret as "a cosy, bijou dwelling ideal for single professionals" whilst any potential tenants would invariably liken the cramped, one-bed apartment to a claustrophobic rabbit hutch with all the appeal of an isolation pod in the Royal Infirmary.

Still riding the post-party wave of adrenalin which followed every successful gig, a wide-awake Miller stashed his cash beneath the sink, stripped to his shorts, and clambered into his single bed with a bottle of fruit-flavoured cider and his laptop intent on downloading a selection of new tracks to his playlist when, assuming the incessant warble of his phone at 2am to be a desperate plea for a fistful of uppers or a bag of weed, he stopped what he was doing and answered succinctly.

'Aye?' he said, as he swigged his cider.

'Jonnie. It's DS Reid. I need a word.'

'Are you joking me? At this time?'

'I can come back with a warrant if you like. We could spend a couple of hours turning your place upside down.'

'Where are you?'

'I'm parked out front. Buzz me in so I don't wake the neighbours.'

* * *

Scaling the stairs two at a time, Duncan, scarcely out of breath, smirked as a semi-naked Miller, barefoot on the landing, ushered him inside.

'I'd offer you a drink,' he said, waving the bottle, 'but this is all I've got.'

'You're alright. I'm on duty.'

'And I'd offer you a seat, but I don't have any chairs.'

'I'll stand.'

'Then watch your head on the ceiling. So, what's so important that it can't wait till the morning?'

'It's about Freya.'

Miller looked at Duncan and frowned.

'Freya?' he said. 'She's not one for trouble. What's she done?'

'You'd best sit down,' said Duncan. 'I'm afraid it's not good news.'

'Oh shite! That's what they say on the telly when someone's had an accident. Is that it? Has she had an accident?'

'Aye. A bad one. There's no easy way of putting this, Jonnie. I'm afraid she's dead.'

Miller slumped to the bed and cocked his head with a look of utter bewilderment on his face.

'Dead?'

'Aye.'

'But she can't be. I mean, she just left the pub a couple of hours ago.'

'Sorry, pal, but she never left the pub. We found her in the ladies.'

'I don't understand. What? What happened?'

'I can't go into details,' said Duncan, 'you know that. All I can say is that she'd been attacked and her bag was stolen, too.'

Miller glanced furtively around the room, swallowed hard, and took another swig from the bottle.

'Are you okay?' said Duncan. 'You look worried.'

'I am worried. You've just told me there's some nutter on the loose.'

'No. I said Freya had been attacked. Is there something you're not telling me? Have you upset someone recently?'

'I make friends, Sergeant. Not enemies.'

'Good. I'm glad to hear it. Now, take a breather, I need to ask you a few questions and think hard before you answer, okay?'

'Aye, okay,' said Miller as he drained the bottle. 'Right then, fire away.'

'Freya. What's her second name?'

'Thomson.'

'I need an address. And a phone number.'

'No bother,' said Miller as he reached for his phone. 'I'll forward it to you now.'

'Good man. Now, did she live alone?'

'No, no. A flat-share with two other girls, Hannah and Sophie.'

'What do they do?'

'Hannah's a courier, Hermes, I think. And Sophie works at the racecourse.'

'The racecourse?' said Duncan. 'Sounds interesting, but I'm not one for a flutter, myself. It's a mug's game.'

'She works at the hotel. Bookings and reservations.'

'And they get on okay? The three of them?'

'As far as I know, aye.'

'And her parents,' said Duncan, 'do you know them?'

Miller blinked twice and wiped his nose with the back of his hand.

'Aye, it's just her mum,' he said. 'She's in Prestwick, St. Cuthbert's Road. Number twenty-two.'

'So, you and Freya,' said Duncan as he scribbled the address in his notebook, 'how long have you two known each other?'

'Since forever. We were at college together.'

'Really? What were you studying?'

'Hospitality, but I never finished the course.'

'How so?'

'I'm not great at writing,' said Miller, 'or concentrating. I never have been.'

'But you remained good friends, even though you dropped out?'

'Aye. Best of pals, we were. It's just a shame she never fancied me like I fancied her.'

'Sometimes it's better that way.'

'Maybe.'

'And how long had she been working for you?'

'No-one works for me,' said Miller, 'not like you mean. I just bung folk a few quid when I need a hand.'

'And is that why she was at the Selkie?'

'Aye. I knew I'd get the place packed to overflowing so I needed someone behind the bar with a wee bit of talent, and Freya's got talent by the bucketload.'

'Well, despite what's happened to Freya, it sounds like you had a good night. Did you have any hassle?'

Miller placed the empty bottle on the floor, wrapped his arms tight around his chest, and stared at Duncan.

'Are you sure she's dead?' he said. 'I mean, are you sure she's not just passed out or something?'

'I'm sure,' said Duncan. 'Now, tell me, was there any trouble in the pub?'

'None. It was a cracking night, everything was sweet.'

'Are you sure about that? Only Tam McDonnell says some fella was trying it on with Freya.'

Miller smiled and shook his head.

'Dancing Dave.'

'Sorry?'

'Dancing Dave, he's dancing daft. If he heard a phone ring, he'd start busting some moves. He's a bit of a cokehead, and he's got two left feet, but he's harmless.'

'So Freya knew him?'

'Aye, of course. He chats her up every time he sees her. It's what some folk call *punching above your weight*.'

'And the rest of your crowd,' said Duncan, 'what are they like? Are they a well-behaved bunch?'

'Aye. They're not interested in fighting, they're into their music.'

'You've quite a following, haven't you?'

'The price of fame, I suppose.'

'So, would you recognise everyone that came to one of your gigs?'

'Pretty much.'

'Could you give me names?'

'Impossible,' said Miller, 'one or two, maybe, but you can't expect me to be on first name terms with a couple of hundred people.'

'Maybe not, but for Freya's sake, I need to know who was at the pub tonight.'

Miller shrugged his shoulders and sighed.

'Sorry,' he said, 'I'd like to help but I don't know how.'

Like an erudite academic struggling with the final clue of a particularly devious cryptic crossword puzzle, Duncan, flummoxed by his predicament, scowled as he slid silently down the wall, settled on his haunches, and scratched the stubble on his cheeks as he desperately sought a solution.

'You're not saying much,' said Miller. 'What are you thinking?'

'I'm thinking you've got a regular following, right?'

'Right.'

'So was there anyone at the Selkie that wasn't a part of your usual mob?'

'Aye, of course, but there's nothing unusual about that. Why?'

'Because,' said Duncan, 'I'm thinking it might easier to identify the folk you're not familiar with than those you are. When's your next gig?'

'Tuesday.'

'Is that not an odd day of the week to be having a party?'

'It's not a big affair,' said Miller. 'It's a warm-up gig for an all-dayer next Friday. I want to see how my tracks go down.'

'An all-dayer on a Friday?'

'It's a Bank Holiday.'

'All right for some, where is it?'

'Raehills Meadows in Moffat.'

'Spreading your wings, aren't you?'

'I go where the music takes me.'

'Very good,' said Duncan with a smile. 'So, your wee gig on Tuesday, where's that?'

'Away! I'm not telling you that! You'd shut me down before I opened the doors!'

'I don't think I'm getting through, am I, Jonnie? See here, pal, Freya's dead and if we don't find the culprit, there's a chance you might be next.'

'Don't be daft,' said Miller, 'why would anyone come after me?'

'Why would anyone go after Freya?'

Miller froze as he pondered the suggestion.

'Just you, right? No police, no uniforms?'

'Just me. You point them out and I'll take it from there.'

'You promise? You're not just saying that?'

'You have my word.'

'Okay. Saltpans Road, on the coast. There's an empty warehouse next to the tyre place.'

'Good. Next question,' said Duncan, 'can you think of anyone that might have had it in for Freya? Doesn't have to be a fella, it could be a girlfriend. Anyone with a grudge? An ex-boyfriend even?'

'No. No-one,' said Miller, 'everyone loved her.'

'And last night, she wasn't acting strangely? You didn't notice anything odd about her behaviour?'

'Nope. She was her usual bubbly self.'

'Talk me through what happened just before she left.'

'Well,' said Miller, 'I announced the last song, she called time, and the punters started drinking up and moving outside. Then she cleared a few tables while I began packing my gear away.'

'She didn't hang around?' said Duncan. 'You didn't have a wee drink or a chat after the show?'

'No. She said she was shattered, and she looked it too. She said she wanted to get off so I said I'd swing by tomorrow to give her her cash.'

'And then she left?'

'Aye, well she said she was going for a pee first so I assumed she must have gone while my back was turned.'

'Was there anyone else left in the pub at that time?'

'Aye, a few.'

'And how long before they left?'

'About another fifteen, twenty minutes. Tam came back soon after.'

'And then you left?'

'No, not straight away. We had a wee natter about how it went, he paid me what he owed, then I left him to it. So, what happens now? With Freya, I mean.'

'I need to visit her next of kin,' said Duncan, 'and fill them in on what's happened, then once they've completed the post-mortem, it'll be up to her parents to arrange the funeral.'

'Can I go?'

'That's not for me to say, but if you and Freya were that close then I see no reason why not. If it's details you're after, then you'd best call her folks but give it a few days. I'm sure they'll be glad to hear from you. Are you okay?'

'Aye. No. I'm not sure,' said Miller. 'I think so. I don't think it's quite sunk in yet.'

'It's often the way,' said Duncan, 'but be prepared, Jonnie, because when it does hit home, it'll hit home hard. If you need to talk to anyone about it, just give me call, we've plenty of folk with years of experience in this kind of thing.'

'I'll bear it in mind.'

'One last thing. I need you to drop by the station tomorrow.'

'What for?'

'I need to get a proper statement off you in full. Half-ten okay?'

'Aye, no bother. If it's for Freya, it's no bother at all.'

Chapter 3

After months of soul-searching followed by a spell on the Holy Isle where life at the retreat was more like a stint in Stalag Luft III than a voyage of self-discovery, Charlotte "Charlie" West had come to the stark realisation that her impetuous behaviour, once regarded as an alluring trait, was in fact fuelled by a typically Taurean sense of impatience which, with the benefit of hindsight, had led her into a disastrous relationship and sent her career spinning off the rails.

However, under the tutelage of her mentor, the retired DI James Munro without whom she would no doubt be living a life of penury and addiction, she'd learned that obstacles were merely stepping stones on the road to success and as a consequence left the emotional trauma of a broken engagement on the streets of London to join him north of the border where she rapidly rose to the rank of Detective Inspector with a reputation for having a bite worse than her bark.

Freed from the crippling lack of confidence which drove her former self to seek solace in a bottle of vodka, a reinvigorated West, clad in tight black jeans and a skinny white tee-shirt, sat with her feet propped on the desk and

gently closed her eyes as she waited patiently for Duncan
to arrive.

* * *

'Not waking you, am I?' he said, as he traipsed through
the door.

'Nope. I was just thinking, that's all.'

'What about?'

'Life,' said West. 'About how good it is up here.'

'If it's all you've ever known,' said Duncan, 'it's really
not that great.'

'Believe me, it is. Did you bring food?'

'Are you joking me? At this time of night? Did you not
have breakfast?'

'To be honest,' said West, 'when you get a call at one in
the morning, breakfast is not the first thing that springs to
mind.'

'No offence,' said Duncan, as he rifled through the
kitchenette, 'but when it comes to food, it's *always* on your
mind. Have we nothing here?'

'I've no idea, I haven't looked.'

'You're in luck, we've half a loaf. I'll pop some toast
on, you make the tea.'

'Sounds like a deal. Are you okay? You look knackered.'

'Probably something to do with the fact I've worked
two shifts already and I've had zero sleep.'

'My heart bleeds,' said West, grinning as she filled the
kettle. 'Maybe we should ask the crims to limit their
activities to the hours of nine to five.'

'It would help.'

'So, what's all this about a girl in a toilet?'

Duncan set a plate of buttered toast on the table and
pulled up a chair.

'Freya Thomson,' he said. 'She was working at The
Bonnie Selkie over on Alloway Street. The owner found
her with a corkscrew in her neck.'

'Ouch! I take it she's…'

'Aye, as a dodo. The weapon hit the jugular and she decorated everything in sight. McLeod's got her on the slab as we speak.'

'What did she do?'

'Barmaid.'

'And the owner?'

'Tam McDonnell,' said Duncan, 'currently a nervous wreck. He'll be along in the morning to give us a full statement.'

'So I take it this Freya girl was one of his staff?'

'No, no. He didn't have any staff, she was a pal of Jonnie Miller's.'

'Miller?'

'Aye. The pub was losing money hand over fist so Miller organised a one-nighter for him and it just about saved him from shutting up shop.'

'Well if Miller's involved, it was only a matter of time before something like this happened.'

'How so?'

'He's a scally!' said West. 'He's up to all sorts!'

'Well I've spoken to him already and he has nothing to do with it.'

'How can you be so sure?'

'Because I know him,' said Duncan, 'he'd not harm a fly.'

'I still say we should bring him in.'

'And give him the third degree? I disagree,' said Duncan. 'To be honest, miss, you need to give the kid a break. He's got learning difficulties.'

'That's no excuse. The fact of the matter is, he's flogging drugs and organising illegal raves.'

'A few pills for his pals and a wee party now and then, it's no big deal. Sometimes you just have to turn a blind eye. Anyway, he had a soft spot for this Thomson girl and he's going to help us identify some possible perps next week.'

West sat back, sipped her tea, and smiled.

'You're beginning to sound like one of those dodgy cops off *Hill Street Blues*.'

'I do my best.'

'What about Tam McDonnell, the owner, what's the SP on him?'

'He moved here from Leith a few months back to open the pub but he couldn't get it off the ground, that's where Miller comes in. He's a nice fella, soft-spoken, about sixty years old, but we'll run him through the PNC all the same.'

'Good. So, what's next?'

Duncan leaned back in his seat, stretched his arms, and sighed.

'Well, first of all,' he said, stifling a yawn, 'we need to inform Freya Thomson's next of kin. They're up in Prestwick.'

'They're going to love you knocking their door in the middle of the night, especially with news like this.'

'Let's face it, miss, if a cop knocks your door in the middle of the night, it's *always* news like this. Then we need to let her flatmates know what's happened, too.'

'Are they nearby?'

'Aye, just over the river. South Beach Road.'

'You'd better get an FLO lined up for her mates as well as her parents.'

'Roger that.'

'What else?'

'McDonnell's in at nine to give his statement and Miller's in straight after. Oh, and there was a pool of vomit by Thomson's body so I've asked McLeod to check whether she might have ingested anything suspicious.'

'You think she may have been spiked?'

'It's a thought,' said Duncan, 'but McLeod's not convinced. He reckons she'd have passed out before she had a chance to puke. Kay Grogan's at the scene, she's got her work cut out for her. She'll drop by once she's through.'

'Is that it?'

'Aye. Apart from a missing bag. Apparently Thomson had one with her but it's gone walkies. I've got uniform combing the area, maybe it was dumped nearby.'

'Well,' said West, as she finished her tea, 'it sounds to me like you've got it covered. I could've stayed in bed.'

'Many hands,' said Duncan. 'I don't suppose you fancy a drive up to Prestwick, do you?'

'Thomson's parents?'

'Aye.'

'Okay,' said West, 'why not. I may as well make myself useful now I'm here.'

'Nice one.'

'Text me the address. Do you want another tea before I go?'

'I'll take a coffee, I need to stay awake. Where's Dougal? It's not like that night owl to be away from his desk.'

'He's gone to Crosshouse.'

'The hospital?'

'Yup. He's interviewing the victim of a robbery.'

'You mean a mugging?'

'No. I mean a robbery,' said West, 'and to be honest, it's just the kind of robbery I wouldn't have minded being involved with myself.'

'I'm hooked. Go on.'

West opened her laptop, looked at Duncan, and winked.

'Whisky,' she said. 'Some shop near Troon. The owner was discovered flat on the floor, out cold, with no sign of any injuries. He came to about a half an hour later.'

'So he just blacked out?'

'Maybe. They're keeping him in for obs just in case he's got some underlying condition. It was only after the ambulance took him away that his assistant noticed a few bottles missing.'

'So we're wasting Dougal's talents on some ned who stole a couple of bottles of whisky?'

'Not just any whisky,' said West. 'Glenfarclas Family Cask. How much do you think it's worth?'

'No idea. Fifty quid? Eighty, maybe?'

'Fourteen thousand, eight hundred.'

Duncan, not normally one to be caught off guard, spluttered as he choked on his toast.

'Are you serious?' he said. 'I could buy a car for that! I could buy two cars!'

'There's more,' said West. 'An Ardbeg, six hundred quid; an eighteen-year-old Lagavulin, four hundred and ninety-five; and get this, a limited edition Bowmore – nineteen thousand, nine hundred and fifty.'

Duncan sat back and scratched the back of his head.

'I suppose that's why they say some folk get drunk on wealth. One thing's for sure, that lot's not going to be easy to shift.'

'Well, they clearly knew what they were after,' said West, 'so I'm guessing they were nicked to order. It's not the kind of haul you'd flog for two and six in some lock-up down a back alley.'

'Aye, I get that,' said Duncan, 'but we should keep an eye on eBay and Gumtree all the same.'

'Dougal's already on it.'

'Well, if you're right, if it was a targeted theft, then maybe the fella was knocked out deliberately. Drugged.'

'Could be,' said West, 'we'll find out as soon as they've done his bloods. There is another option of course, if they threatened him he could have keeled over with the shock.'

'I take it if they're carrying stock like that in their shop then they'll have cameras all over the place?'

'Yup, everywhere. Dougal's downloaded the footage already, he'll bring it back with him.'

'So, we've got our hands full again?'

'When haven't we?'

'It's a shame the chief's not here,' said Duncan, 'he's always willing to pitch in.'

'He might be a volunteer, Duncan, but he's retired and he needs to take a step back. I think the new house is keeping him busy.'

'The house? So he's down in Auchencairn? I thought that place needed gutting.'

'It does. He's kipping on a Z-bed and cooking off a camping stove. He seems to be enjoying himself.'

'Until he gets wind of this.'

'He won't,' said West, 'because we're not going to tell him.'

'We won't have to,' said Duncan. 'You know Munro – when it comes to bodies, he's like a cadaver dog in a cemetery.'

Chapter 4

As an introverted alpha geek who preferred the company of the internet to exchanging idle gossip with colleagues, friends, or family, DS Dougal McCrae – blessed with the ability to hack a computer with the speed of a malevolent virus – was happiest when working in the solitude of an empty office, the upside to his social anxiety being an enviable amount of disposable income which, much to the chagrin of his girlfriend, allowed him to indulge his passion for all things Italian rather than splurge on a romantic dinner for two at a fancy restaurant.

Assigned with the task of interviewing the victim of what appeared to be an opportunistic robbery, he reluctantly zipped his Brioni blouson to the neck, mounted his Vespa GTS, and hurtled along a deserted A77 like a *ragazzo figo* in search of gelato to meet with the pensionable Charles Bewley who, despite his ordeal, was found relaxing in an armchair in the Combined Assessment Unit of Crosshouse Hospital perusing a well-worn copy of *Scottish Field* magazine.

The seventy-six-year-old balding connoisseur – dressed in a tweed blazer, brown corduroys, and polished Oxford brogues – sat with the authoritative air of an ageing professor studying a woeful dissertation on the influence of the Renaissance on English literature when, alerted by the swish of the curtain draped around his bay room, he closed the magazine, raised his head, and peered over the rim of his tortoiseshell spectacles.

'You don't look like a doctor to me,' he said, sternly.

'Police officer,' said Dougal. 'Charles Bewley?'

'The one and only.'

'DS McCrae, sir. I'm here about your accident.'

'Do you have any identification?'

'I have,' said Dougal, as he produced his badge. 'Are you up for a wee chat?'

'As long it's meaningful and informative. I've no time for banter.'

'You and me both. How are you feeling?'

'First class,' said Bewley. 'They've checked my BP, completed an ECG, and taken several pints of blood for testing but thus far they can find nothing wrong.'

'Well, maybe the bloods will reveal something but apart from that, you're okay?'

'The only thing I'm suffering from, young man, is an acute case of severe boredom so I'll leave it to you to administer some relief. Ask me some questions. As many as you like.'

Dougal placed his helmet on the bed, produced a notepad, and closed the curtain.

'Right you are,' he said. 'How about we start with you telling me exactly what happened, as you remember it.'

'Very well,' said Bewley. 'I was standing in the shop—'

'Alone?'

'If you're going to interrupt my every word, we're not going to get very far, are we?'

'Sorry.'

'As I was saying, I was standing in the shop, *alone*, dusting down the bottles on the shelves—'

'What time was this?'

Bewley rolled his eyes and huffed.

'8:35pm,' he said. 'Approximately.'

'Is that not a wee bit late for a shop like you to be open?'

'I remain open until ten. There's often a rush in the evening with folk of certain calibre in search of a pocket-friendly tipple.'

'I see,' said Dougal. 'So it's not just the expensive stuff you sell?'

'Indeed not. I keep a limited selection of affordable but palatable whiskies too. The Famous Grouse, Glenfiddich, that kind of thing.'

'Okay. So it's just after half-eight and you're alone in the shop. What happened next?'

'A young man entered,' said Bewley. 'He was after a Macallan. I showed him what I had but he was rather taken by one of the ones I keep behind the glass.'

'A decent one, was it?'

'Very. An Estate Reserve. Three hundred and ninety-nine pounds. He contemplated the purchase and said he'd return after a quick discussion with his wife.'

'That's a rarity.'

'I think he was concerned about how much he'd be allowed to spend.'

'Can you describe him for me?'

'I'll try,' said Bewley. 'Six feet tall, slim build, clean cut, brown hair, well turned out.'

'Very good. So he popped outside?'

'He did. As he left, two paramedics came in. A man and a woman.'

'I hope they weren't on a shout,' said Dougal. 'How were they?'

'Polite. Friendly. They seemed, shall we say, *close*.'

'Can you explain?'

'They were touching and smiling in a way only those involved in a relationship would do.'

'I see.'

'They said they'd ended their shift and were looking for something a little special. A birthday gift for the lady's father.'

'And did you manage to entice them?'

'I did,' said Bewley. 'A Tamdhu single malt.'

'I've not heard of it. Is that one of your pocket-friendly types?'

'That all depends on the size of your pockets. Seventy-five pounds.'

'I think I'll stick with the Irn-Bru. So, was that them away?'

'I assume so. I didn't actually see them leave. I gift-wrapped the box and then...'

Bewley's words tailed off as he frowned and shook his head.

'Damn and blast!' he said. 'That's all I can remember! I gift-wrapped the box and was handing it over just as the other fellow came back and the next thing I know, Morag's hovering over me like the angel of death muttering something about an ambulance being on its way.'

'I'm not being funny,' said Dougal, 'but that's the epitome of bad luck, fainting when the two paramedics were leaving.'

'Indeed.'

'So you've no idea what this other fella did?'

'I've no idea. Perhaps he tried to help. Perhaps he alerted Morag to my predicament. Perhaps it was he who called the ambulance. I really don't know.'

'No bother,' said Dougal, 'we'll try and track him down. This Morag you mention, is she your wife?'

'I'm what you might call a confirmed bachelor. Morag is my constant companion and personal assistant.'

'Has she told you about the missing whisky?'

'I haven't got the details but suffice to say I knew I had insurance for a reason.'

'How long has she been working for you?'

'Years,' said Bewley. 'Sixteen to be precise.'

'So she's a reliable sort? Trustworthy?'

'Utterly.'

'Is she here?'

'I sent her on her way,' said Bewley. 'I'm not one for people fussing over me, I can cope perfectly well on my own.'

'So she's gone home?'

'She said she'd rather wait for me at the shop.'

'Not being funny,' said Dougal, 'but should you not be getting some rest instead of going back to work?'

'I'm wide awake,' said Bewley. 'The last thing I need right now is rest. Besides, I'd quite like to see what damage has been done and make sure the place is secure.'

'Well, if she's at the shop, I'll drop by in a wee while and take a look for myself. Tell me, Mr Bewley, how's security at your place?'

'Perfectly adequate. Impenetrable locks, steel shutters, that sort of thing.'

'Do you have any security cameras?'

'Indeed we do.'

'Good. And how's the footage from your cameras stored? Is it backed up by a third party?'

'No. It's recorded and stored on the system in the office.'

'Okay, I'll need to download that and take it with me,' said Dougal. 'Is that alright with you?'

'Perfectly.'

'Will I need a password to access your computer?'

'Morag will see to that.'

'Excellent. Well, I'm almost done for now, Mr Bewley. No doubt we'll be speaking again but before I go, were there any other customers earlier the day?'

'A few,' said Bewley. 'A handful of people came and went, tourists mainly, here for the golf I imagine.'

'And would you say they were normal? Nothing suspicious about them?'

'They were American. Enough said.'

'And how were you feeling during the day?' said Dougal. 'Health-wise, I mean.'

'One hundred percent. Why?'

'I was wondering if you'd had any dizzy spells. Fainting like that is often caused by low blood sugar or by simply not eating enough.'

'Despite your sage advice, I can assure you I had a hearty breakfast followed by a rather substantial lunch, which reminds me, I hope Morag's had the foresight to put my supper on.'

Dougal stood, returned the notebook to his inside pocket, and tucked his helmet under his arm.

'I'll remind her when I get there,' he said. 'Best of luck, Mr Bewley. I'll be in touch.'

* * *

As the only shop glowing on an otherwise dormant West Portland Street, Bewley's World of Whisky – a quaint, bay-fronted shop with a distinctly Dickensian feel – oozed the welcoming charm of a hostelry in the nether regions of the Highlands.

Wary of spooking a lone female at one in the morning, Dougal removed his helmet, tapped gently on the door, and smiled as he pressed his warrant card against the window.

'Police Scotland,' he said, trying not shout. 'I'm here about the robbery.'

A lady of a certain age wearing a figure-hugging black dress more suited to a soirée than serving customers, eyed Dougal with a degree of suspicion as she eased open the door.

'Police, you say?'

'Aye. DS Dougal McCrae.'

'Aren't you a little young to be a detective?'

'I'm old enough.'

'Where's your car?'

Dougal flicked his head towards his scooter.

'I prefer two wheels,' he said. 'I've just come from the hospital. Mr Bewley's doing fine and he says you're to put his supper on.'

'You'd best come in.'

As someone whose inherent shyness was directly to blame for his lack of experience with members of the opposite sex, Dougal – intimidated in particular by those who flaunted their sexuality with the brazen cheek of a luckless hussy – felt the beads of sweat gathering on his forehead as she sashayed slowly across the floor and leaned seductively against the counter.

'It's late,' she said as she brushed a lick of dyed blonde hair from her forehead. 'Can I get you anything?'

'No, you're alright,' said Dougal, quaking in his boots. 'I need to crack on, if that's okay with you.'

'Of course. How can I help?'

'First of all, I'll need your full name please, madam.'

'Miss.'

'Sorry. Miss.'

'Morag Fleming.'

'Fleming? So, you and Mr Bewley, you're not married?'

'No. Which has left something of a void in my life, if you know what I mean.'

'Aye, I get the drift. So, what exactly is your relationship?'

'I'm his constant companion, his confidante, his book-keeper, his PA, and his cleaner.'

'Do you live nearby?'

'Charles and I share a delightfully large house on Henderson Road. It's not far.'

'It must have been quite a shock finding him like that.'

'It was awful,' said Fleming, 'I thought he'd had a heart attack and died.'

'And do you remember roughly what time it was when you found him?'

'Oh, I'm not sure. About nine, I think. Give or take.'

'And the shop,' said Dougal, 'was it empty?'

'It was, but the front door was ajar. People these days, you'd think they were born in a barn.'

'So, you saw Mr Bewley lying on the floor, what did you do next?'

'Well, naturally I ran to his aid,' said Fleming. 'He wasn't dead after all, thank God. I could see he was breathing. I placed my hand on his chest and I could feel his heart beating but he was out cold. That's when I called the ambulance.'

'And did the crew mention anything about his condition?'

'No. He was just waking up, they checked his pulse, asked him a couple of questions, then put an oxygen mask on his face and carted him off.'

'And you followed?'

'Not immediately,' said Fleming. 'I couldn't. I had to make sure everything was locked up. That's when I noticed the cabinet.'

Fleming raised an arm and pointed towards an antique, glass-fronted display unit.

'What about it?' said Dougal.

'It was open, some bottles were missing and that's when I realised we'd been robbed.'

'And were the items stolen of significant value?'

'I'd say thirty-six thousand pounds' worth of stock was quite significant, Sergeant, wouldn't you?'

'So you called the police?'

'I did.'

'Can you give me a list of what was taken?'

'I most certainly can. I'll write it down for you.'

Dougal, intrigued to see that the door had not been forced nor the glass broken, wandered over for a closer look and turned to face Fleming as she handed him the list.

'I take it this thing's normally locked, is that right?'

'Absolutely.'

'So who has the key?'

'There's one in the office and Charles keeps the other on his key ring.'

'Then it seems reasonable to assume that Mr Bewley must have opened it for someone?'

Fleming shrugged her shoulders.

'Probably,' she said. 'I really don't know.'

'Tell me,' said Dougal, 'while all this was going on out here, where were you exactly?'

'In the cellar. Stock-taking.'

'On a Saturday night?'

'We always do it on a Saturday, then we place an order to replenish stock on the Sunday. Online. We've a wholesaler in Glasgow.'

'But that's not for the expensive stuff?'

'No,' said Fleming. 'Charles buys that in person, more often than not, direct from the distilleries.'

'So once you'd finished in the cellar, you came up here?'

'I came up, made a pot of tea, and that's when I found him.'

'And as you say, the shop was empty?'

Fleming nodded.

'And once you'd locked up, you headed for the hospital?'

'I wish I hadn't bothered,' said Fleming. 'He's not one for expressing his gratitude, is Charles. No sooner had I arrived than he told me to bugger off.'

'Let's move on,' said Dougal. 'I understand you've a good security system here?'

'It's good enough.'

'It's your cameras I'm interested in. I can't see them.'

'There's two. They're outside above the door.'

'No offence,' said Dougal, 'but they're not much use out there.'

'We're a wee whisky shop, Sergeant. Not a bank.'

'Aye, but you're selling high-value goods.'

'Which is why the cabinet is alarmed and we've a panic button beneath the counter.'

'Well, that's something, I suppose,' said Dougal. 'I'm going to need a copy of the footage from your cameras for the whole of Saturday, can you do that for me?'

Fleming smiled and winked at Dougal.

'I can do anything you like, Sergeant. Follow me.'

Dougal averted his eyes as Fleming wiggled her way to the office where an LCD display took pride of place on an oak desk, the screen covered in a patchwork of images displaying different areas of the shop. Bending in an unnecessarily exaggerated manner, she leaned across the desk and tapped away at the keyboard before coyly looking over her shoulder.

'Shall I put it on a stick for you?'

'Ideal,' said Dougal, nervously. 'A stick's ideal.'

'It'll take a moment or two. Are you sure I can't get you anything?'

'Just the footage. Thanks.'

Fleming logged off, shimmied as she straightened her dress, and passed it over.

'Thanks very much,' said Dougal. 'I may need to speak to you again.'

'Anytime. You're welcome to call at the house if you prefer, it's very private.'

'I'll bear it in mind,' said Dougal as he headed for the street. 'Don't forget to lock your doors.'

Chapter 5

Unlike his anaemic colleague who was genetically predisposed to function at his peak during the hours of darkness, Duncan – favouring a good night's sleep and a healthy tan to the peely-wally complexion of a Beluga whale – jumped from his seat as Dougal blew through the door like a caffeine addict on a double ristretto.

'Look at me!' he said, slamming his helmet on the desk. 'I'm sweating!'

'Calm your jets, pal. What the hell are you havering about?'

'Morag Fleming! She's a man-eater!'

Duncan stretched his arms and scratched the back of his head.

'Well, if you've got to go,' he said, 'that's the way to do it. So, who exactly is this Morag Fleming?'

'The whisky fella's partner.'

'Oh aye, the whisky. Westy mentioned that. Quite a haul by the sounds of it.'

'It was,' said Dougal. 'Nearly forty grand's worth.'

'He'll not be happy about that. Is he still in the hospital?'

'Aye, but he's okay. He just fainted, it's no surprise given his age.'

'What's he like?'

'He's a toff,' said Dougal, 'with a big plum in his mouth. He must've gone to Gordonstoun or somewhere like that, I mean, how else would folk learn about whisky?'

Duncan shrugged his shoulders and smiled.

'You're asking the wrong fella,' he said. 'Where I grew up, folk thought you were posh if you used a glass for your Buckie. So, have you got any leads?'

'Aye, one fella just now. I've got some CCTV to go through. I'm hoping I can get a decent still off the footage so we can ID him.'

'Can you not track him along the street?'

'I'm not sure yet. There's only one camera and that's at the junction with Templehill so unless he was headed in that direction, we're pretty much humped. Why are you here anyway? Should you not be in your bed?'

'I should, aye,' said Duncan, 'but a wee dead girl put paid to that.'

'Are you joking me? When did this happen?'

'Late last night. She was working at the Selkie. Never made it home.'

'Oh, that's tragic,' said Dougal. 'Pure tragic. Not a youngster, was she?'

'Aye. Mid-twenties or thereabouts. Lassie by the name of Freya Thomson; she had her throat cut.'

'That's plenty. You know what I'm like when it comes to blood.'

'Your Kay's on the scene. She said she'd drop by when she's done.'

'She'll be wanting breakfast then.'

'She's not the only one.'

'Where's Westy? If we've a body on our hands then surely she should be here.'

'She was,' said Duncan. 'She volunteered to break the bad news to Thomson's next of kin.'

'Oh, I don't envy her that. What are you up to then?'

'I'm away to see Thomson's flatmates in a while. I need to give her place the once over, too. Then the pub owner's coming in to give his statement followed by Jonnie Miller.'

'Miller? He's coming here? Of his own accord?'

'Aye. Freya Thomson's one of his pals,' said Duncan. 'He's going to help us out. Right, I need another coffee. Are you wanting one?'

'Yes please,' said Grogan as she humped her bags through the door. 'And a bacon roll, heavy on the ketchup.'

* * *

As the archetypal girl next door, Kay Grogan could have had her pick of the beer-swilling, testosterone-laden lads willing to throw themselves at her feet were it not for the fact that overt displays of Neanderthal masculinity was about as attractive as the prospect of root canal surgery without an anaesthetic whereas the inquisitive mind of the bookish DS Dougal McCrae was, by contrast, as stimulating as an aphrodisiac.

'That was fun,' she said, beaming. 'Have you heard from McLeod yet?'

'No, no. It's too soon for that,' said Duncan. 'You're looking pleased with yourself. What have you got?'

'Plenty,' said Grogan. 'And I've a wee surprise for you, too.'

'Well, it's not my birthday but I'll gladly accept. Shoot.'

'Fingerprints.'

'You got some?'

'I got hundreds but they're not much use. There's too many and they're mostly partial.'

'I'm not surprised,' said Duncan. 'After all, it's a public toilet.'

'Aye, but one thing a public toilet has that works for me, is a tiled floor. Latent footprints. They show up a treat.'

'Go on.'

'They're all over the place but I got one from inside the cubicle just by the girl's body and it's a belter.'

Grogan pulled her phone from her pocket, opened an image, and passed it to Duncan.

'I took this with the FLS shining on the floor. What does that tell you?'

'Sorry, hen, I'm not a foot-ologist and I'm suffering from sleep deprivation, you'll have to help me out here.'

'One: the imprint is almost perfect. There's little or no wear to the heel or toe which means they're practically brand new. Two: the tread is unique, it's off a Doc Marten. And three: get this, it's in the wrong place.'

'What do you mean?'

'For a start,' said Grogan, 'it's facing the wall, not the door, and it's by the side of the pan, not in front of it.'

'Well maybe the lassie dropped something on the floor and turned around to pick it up.'

'Aye, maybe,' said Grogan, 'but there's not many women I know that take a size ten. I reckon it belongs to the perp. I got a palm print too, off the back wall. Right hand, about four feet up.'

Duncan, eyes widening as the penny dropped, leapt to his feet, swung a chair against the wall, and placed a foot beside it.

'So, you're thinking the perp sort of straddled the bowl like this, bracing himself against the wall with his right hand as he lifted Thomson onto the pan with his left?'

'Something like that.'

'Okay, I'm six foot. Is my hand in the right place?'

'No. Too high,' said Grogan.

'Dougal, you try.'

Dougal crossed the floor, adopted a similar stance, and glanced back at Grogan.

'I'm five seven and a half,' he said. 'How's that?'

'Spot on.'

Duncan returned the chair to the desk and smiled at Grogan.

'You're a doll,' he said. 'So, margin for error, we're after a fella around five-seven to five-nine, wearing a pair of size-ten Docs.'

'I'd say so. If I'm right.'

'If you're right,' said Duncan, 'you're in the wrong job. Come Tuesday, this is going to make my job a whole lot easier.'

'What's happening on Tuesday?'

'I'm attending a wee party and with any luck, this fella's going to be there, too.'

'Good luck,' said Grogan, glancing at her watch. 'Right, I need to get a move on, I've got to get my findings up to Glasgow and get them analysed but before I go, here's your wee gift.'

Grogan took a pair of blue, latex gloves and a sealed plastic pouch from her bag of tricks and slid them across the table.

'Uniform said you were looking for this.'

'Is that Thomson's bag?'

'I think so, and I'm assuming you'll be wanting me to take a look at it, too.'

'Aye, just bear with me, hen, and it's all yours.'

Duncan snapped on the gloves and shook his head as he unzipped the bag.

'No, no,' he said. 'This isn't right. This isn't right at all!'

'What's up?'

'Somebody stole this bag and dumped it, right?'

'Apparently,' said Grogan. 'They found it in a waste bin at the edge of the car park.'

'So who,' said Duncan, as he tipped the contents to the table, 'would steal a handbag and not take the mobile phone? Or the car key? Or the purse containing forty quid, a bank card, and two credit cards?'

'Maybe he panicked,' said Dougal. 'You know, if someone saw him with the bag and gave chase, maybe he dumped it before he had a chance to look inside.'

Duncan clasped his hands behind his head, leaned back in his seat, and stared vacuously into space as he contemplated an alternative scenario.

'I'm not convinced,' he said. 'It's a wee bag. It's not as if he was running with a heavy rucksack.'

'I get that,' said Dougal, 'but if someone was on his tail the last thing he'd want is to get caught with it in his possession.'

Duncan turned to Grogan and frowned.

'Remember what McLeod said? That she was facing her attacker?'

'Aye?'

'And that she put up a struggle?'

'Aye?'

'Well maybe he wasn't interested in any of this. Maybe she had something else in her bag. Something worth hanging on to?'

'Maybe,' said Grogan. 'But what?'

'I've no idea,' said Duncan, 'and I'm too tired to get my head round it just now. Look, I'll hang on to the phone, you take the rest. Dust everything and if you find anything, let me know as soon as you can.'

Blushing as Grogan fired him the subtlest of winks, Dougal lowered his head and set about downloading the security camera footage to his desktop while Duncan toyed with Thomson's phone.

With just a handful of texts exchanged between herself and Jonnie Miller, the most recent being less than a day old, a few selfies taken in her bedroom, and a call log listing only two incoming calls in the last seven days, an increasingly frustrated Duncan – surprised that anyone who worked in hospitality could lead such a sheltered life – headed for the kitchen.

'I can't concentrate,' he said. 'Dougal, do me a favour, pal. Fetch yourself a pair of gloves.'

'Gloves?'

'Aye. I need you to take a look at this phone.'

'Oh, I'd love to but I've got all this footage to go through.'

'Listen, pal, my murder trumps your whisky. It'll not take long for a genius like you.'

'Aye okay, then. What is it you're after?'

'Go through the list of contacts. I'm needing names and addresses of anyone we don't know about. And see if you can retrieve any deleted messages. You never know, maybe she was hiding something.'

Dougal sat back, crossed his legs, and sighed as he scrolled through the list like a bored telly addict fumbling with the remote control.

'Either she's not fussed about predictive text,' he said, 'or she speaks a different language to the rest of us.'

'What do you mean?'

'Well, I've got some obvious ones here; *Mum, Jonnie, Sophie, Hannah—*'

'That's her flatmates.'

'—but the rest make no sense at all; *Drout, Dugs, Rab, Windaes.*'

Duncan glanced at Dougal and smiled.

'As you're a teetotal,' he said, 'I'll forgive you your ignorance. They're all pubs. Drouthy Neebors, The Twa Dugs, Rabbies Bar, and the Wee Windaes.'

'I'd never have guessed.'

'You need to get out more. She must've been working them too. I'll swing by when I'm done with McDonnell and Miller.'

* * *

Preferring the printed word to any visual form of entertainment, Dougal, unable to tell a PlayStation from an Xbox or a Game Boy from a Stadia, nonetheless likened

50

the screening of surveillance footage to a real-life video game in which players were tasked with unearthing clues in a bid to hunt down the suspects.

With only a clutch of touristy types patronising Bewley's World of Whisky during the day, he focused excitedly on the same fifteen-minute period of footage surrounding the robbery, eagerly rewinding, zooming, scrutinising and capturing stills of the "Macallan man" and the two paramedics, pausing only for the occasional glug of Irn-Bru.

'No Duncan?' said West, as she returned to the office.

'You've just missed him,' said Dougal. 'He's gone to see the dead girl's flatmates.'

'Shame. I just bought him a bumper breakfast, too. The poor bloke deserves it.'

'I think I may have earned the right to a wee snack myself.'

'I don't doubt it,' said West, 'but you haven't done a double shift. Not yet, anyway. Sausage or bacon?'

'I'll take a bacon,' said Dougal. 'How did you get on?'

'Alright, I suppose,' said West, 'but it never gets any easier, does it? Telling some poor sod they're never going to see their daughter again.'

'No. It does not. Maybe the family liaison officer will help them get through it.'

'They declined the offer. It's no big deal, some people are better at dealing with stuff on their own. Did you get anywhere with that Bewley bloke from the whisky shop?'

'Aye, I got what I could. Are you up for a wee swatch of the video?'

'Yup, what have you got?'

Dougal took a bite of his buttie, dusted off his fingers, and flipped the screen to face West.

'Right,' he said, 'there's only two cameras, they're outside by the front door. According to Bewley this fella came in, he had his eye on a Macallan.'

'Well dressed,' said West. 'He looks like he earns a bob or two.'

'He probably does. Bewley said he took a shine to one of the expensive bottles then stepped outside to make a call. He thought he was calling his wife. As he steps out, this ambulance pulls up and two paramedics go inside. But here's the thing, the fella after the Macallan doesn't make a call, he doesn't even have a phone, and he's not speaking to anyone so he's not on hands-free.'

'Well, maybe he said he was making a call as an excuse,' said West. 'Bought himself some time to ponder his decision without embarrassing himself.'

'Aye, maybe,' said Dougal, 'but then he goes back inside, reappears exactly four seconds later, turns left down the street, and disappears around the corner. The paramedics come out a few minutes later, you can see the lassie's carrying a gift bag.'

'Well, that bloke, the one you call the Macallan man, he's wearing an overcoat. He could have stuffed the bottles in his pockets when no-one was looking.'

'He could have,' said Dougal, rewinding the tape, 'but look at his coat. No bulges. Even if he used the inside pockets, his coat would be hanging heavy on his shoulders.'

'So what are you thinking?'

'I'm not sure,' said Dougal, 'but I thought, what if he was wearing something under his coat to carry the bottles?'

'You mean like a gilet? Or a fisherman's waistcoat?'

'Aye.'

'You've got to hand it to him if he was,' said West. 'Clever thinking. What about the paramedics?'

'They bought a pricey bottle of malt for the girl's father. They don't look fussed by anything so I can only assume they never saw the other fella lift the bottles.'

'You should have a word, anyway.'

'I'm already on it,' said Dougal. 'The ambulance is a Honda CR-V 2.2 i-DTEC. The index shows up clear as a bell: Sierra, Echo, six, seven, Delta, November, Echo. They probably came from Crosshouse so they'll be easy to trace.'

'Nice one,' said West. 'Well, as Duncan's not here it would be a shame to let these go cold, do you want another?'

'Aye, go on. Same again, please. Have you heard from the boss at all? I still can't get used to him not being here.'

'He's tied up with the new house. Silly bugger'll probably do himself a mischief but he's refusing to get any help until he gets to the serious stuff.'

Chapter 6

Although the sale of the terraced whitewashed cottage was common knowledge amongst the curious villagers of Auchencairn, for the audacious few brazen enough to peek unashamedly through the dusty sash windows, the sight of a duvet strewn across a Z-bed, a saucepan sitting atop a camping stove, and a small dog running wild around the lounge, was enough to convince them that the new owner was someone of insufficient means.

Regarded as something of an enigma by the dozen or so locals he'd encountered face to face – all of whom assumed the stern-faced gent with piercing blue eyes to be an ex-serviceman or a merciless sheriff at the county court – the retired Detective Inspector James Munro had, in an effort to protect his privacy, informed them that he was in fact a professional embalmer on sabbatical, a yarn which had thus far kept the prying tattlers from his door.

As a childless widower – his beloved Jean having passed some years earlier – Munro, fearful that without a will the Crown would inherit, auction-off, and ultimately profit from the sale of his worldly goods, had decided to invest his meagre savings in the run-down property not for financial gain but for the simple pleasure of bequeathing it to the scatter-brained Charlie West in the hope that, once settled, the daughter he'd never had might focus not so much on her career but on starting a family with somebody strong enough to cope with her demanding personality.

Well aware that the downside to owning a house hewn from granite was, in the absence of central heating, the fact that the temperature indoors was permanently akin to that of the ice-box in the refrigerator, Munro fired up the wood burner, turned on the radio, and set about demolishing a stud wall, muttering to himself as Murdo, his Scottish terrier, looked on attentively.

'There are some folk who say you should know your limitations. I say if you want a job done properly, you should do it yourself.'

With his infallible canine instinct alerting him to an imminent disaster, the dog scurried beneath the bed as Munro, diving for cover, narrowly avoided being struck on the head by a falling sheet of plasterboard.

'One down,' he said proudly, 'three to go.'

Impressed by the speed with which the house was caving-in around him, he stopped to brush the dust particles from his balding pate just as the hourly bulletin for Dumfries and Galloway came on air which, aside from the usual updates on road closures and fundraising events, was made all the more interesting for the mention of a fatality in the Moffat area described by police as *suspicious*, an occurrence rare enough to have him reaching for his phone.

* * *

As a young, green, and worryingly hapless detective based in Dumfries, Greg Byrne would have undoubtedly faced disciplinary action as a result of his negligent if not incompetent behaviour during the course of his first ever murder investigation under the rank of Inspector were it not for Munro's serendipitous involvement in the case.

However, with a string of successful though minor convictions under his belt, he'd finally managed to bolster his sense of self-worth and save himself from demotion.

'Mr Munro!' he said, excitedly. 'This is a surprise, are you okay?'

'Aye, not bad. And yourself?'

'Couldn't be better!'

'How are you getting on?' said Munro. 'Have you settled into your new role, yet?'

'Oh aye, like a hand in glove. I know I've said it before, but if it wasn't for your–'

'Och, wheesht! All you needed was a nudge in the right direction, that's all.'

'A kick in the backside, more like, not that I'm complaining. So, have you something on your mind?'

'No, no. It's just a courtesy call,' said Munro. 'I've a few minutes before I head out.'

'Anywhere nice?'

'Moffat. I've a dear friend I've not seen in months so I thought I'd pay him a visit.'

'Well, allow yourself some extra time,' said Byrne, 'you might hit some traffic.'

'Nonsense. There's never any traffic in Moffat.'

'There might be today. We're dealing with an incident just now.'

'Is that so? A couple of boy racers involved in an RTC no doubt.'

'It's not that exciting,' said Byrne. 'A fella's fallen from some scaffolding.'

'Then you'll have Health and Safety on your back, too. If you dinnae mind me asking, when did this happen?'

'No idea yet,' said Byrne, 'but we got the call just a couple of hours ago.'

'And the gentleman in question, is he…?'

'Put it this way, Mr Munro, if you're at all religious you'd do well to light a few candles for the repose of his soul.'

'Dear, dear, dear. In that case, perhaps I ought to postpone my trip.'

'No need,' said Byrne. 'If you loop around and approach Moffat from the north, you'll be alright. The incident's about ten miles further south, on the Raehills Estate.'

'Then I shall take your advice,' said Munro. 'Tell me, are you not attending the scene yourself?'

'With all due respect, it's an accident, Mr Munro. Not a murder. I've a DC on the case.'

'Well, you've probably got enough on your plate as it is. I should be off or I'll be late. I'm glad to hear you're okay.'

'Thanks very much,' said Byrne. 'You take care now, no doubt we'll be speaking soon.'

'Sooner than you think,' said Munro as he ended the call. 'Right, Murdo, we're away a walk and I think Raehills sounds like the ideal place for you to stretch your legs.'

* * *

Favoured by Sunday drivers who looked forward to the prospect of tailing a Massey Ferguson at twenty miles an hour in order to justify their pedestrian pace, the road from Dumfries to Moffat, flanked by fields and coniferous woodland, offered spectacular views of some of south-west Scotland's most picturesque countryside, but for Munro, who was as familiar with the landscape as he was with his own reflection, the sight of an empty carriageway held more appeal.

Lowering the visor against the dazzling morning sun, he floored the accelerator intent on reaching Moffat as fast as his ageing Peugeot would carry him.

Slowing to a crawl as he spotted the blue and white cordon stretched across the approach road to the estate, he flashed his headlights at the constable on duty, gave a subtle wave, and mounted the verge.

Vindicating his intentions with the caveat that an officer is never off duty, not even retired ones, Munro, willing to accept the consequences for pushing the boundaries of acceptable behaviour if a suspected murderer was at large, opened the glove box, retrieved a baseball cap emblazoned with a band of Sillitoe tartan around the rim, and pulled it low over his brow.

'Right,' he said, leaving Murdo in the car, 'in for a penny.'

Like an irate bounty hunter pouncing on his prey, he stormed towards the officer, scowling as he jabbed his finger in the air.

'You, laddie! Who's the SIO here?'

The young officer, clearly intimidated, stepped to one side and raised the cordon.

'DC Clark, sir! Straight up the lane.'

Relieved at clearing the first hurdle, Munro, allowing himself a wry grin, stopped to admire Raehills House, a magnificent eighteenth-century Tudor-style mansion surrounded by ornamental gardens set in five hundred acres of unadulterated woodland, the only blot on the landscape being the temporary music stages in various phases of construction dotted about the meadows where a young man, conspicuous by his attire, sat wiping mud from his Timberland boots.

With a carefully coiffed mane of straw blonde hair and a tailored, dark blue suit, DC Daniel Clark – more sales assistant than senior investigating officer – raised his head as a curmudgeonly old man marched towards him.

'I'm looking for Clark!'

'That's me,' said the DC, as he shoved the tissue into his pocket.

'Have you nothing to do?'

'I'm waiting on SOCOs and a pathologist.'

'And in the meantime all you can do is buff your shoes?'

'Well, I was just–'

'I'm sure you were! We'll see what DI Byrne has to say about this, he's on his way over now.'

Unnerved by Munro's forthright if not threatening behaviour, Clark nonetheless plucked up the courage to ask the inevitable question.

'Not being funny,' he said, 'but I've not seen you before. Can I ask your name?'

Munro, feigning umbrage at the question, leaned forward and punctuated his reply with the briefest of pauses.

'D... I... Munro,' he said, gritting his teeth. 'Any more questions?'

'No. You're alright,' said Clark, nervously. 'That's fine.'

'What's going on here?'

'They're getting ready for a music festival, sir. It's this weekend.'

'So, what have we got?'

Clark pointed at a body lying supine by the stage and took a deep breath.

'Male, IC1,' he said. 'He's stone cold. I reckon he's about twenty-five, twenty-six years old and about five-ten tall. I think he fell from the lighting rig.'

Munro clasped his hands behind his back as his eyes darted from the body to the rig and back again.

'If he'd fallen during the day,' he said, 'his colleagues would've been with him but looking at the state of the fellow, it's clear to see he's been here all night. The question is what was he doing here after hours, on his own?'

'I've no idea, sir.'

'Have you contacted the firm he works for?'

'We're still trying to find that out,' said Clark. 'My pal's making enquiries up at the house.'

'But he wasn't discovered until this morning?'

'That's correct.'

'So what does that tell you?'

'Well, obviously, that he was alone,' said Clark. 'He must've been working late, maybe he just wanted to get the job done.'

Munro, already riled by Clark's apathy concerning the circumstances surrounding the young man's death, looked to the clear, blue sky and raised a hand to shield his eyes from the sun.

'What was the temperature like last night?'

'Not that great,' said Clark. 'It was warm enough by day but it dropped to five or six degrees in the town. It's quite exposed here so I'd say it was probably much colder than that.'

'And yet,' said Munro, 'he's wearing just a tee-shirt. Was there nae coat to be found?'

'We've not done a search of the area yet, sir. Maybe there's a jacket lying about at the back of the stage.'

'And no vehicles?'

'Sorry?'

'For crying out loud, laddie! A car, or a van! He must have got here somehow!'

'No,' said Clark, sheepishly. 'No vehicles.'

'Which would lead you to believe, what?'

Clark hesitated before answering.

'That he must have arrived with someone during the day and got left behind? Or maybe he'd arranged to get a lift home with somebody else later? A taxi, even?'

Bemused by the lack of ladders, key clamps, or cabling attached to the rig, Munro stepped up to the scaffolding and ran a finger along one of the poles.

'Rain?' he said, wiping the water from his hands.

'I'm not with you,' said Clark.

'Did it rain last night?'

'No. Dry as a bone.'

'But there was a heavy dew. It's damp under foot and the scaffolding's wet.'

'Aye! I saw that,' said Clark, trying to redeem himself. 'That's why I'm thinking he slipped and fell.'

'Wrong answer,' said Munro.

'How so?'

'Because the poor chap's stiff as a board which means he expired several hours ago. There was no dew when he hit the ground.'

'Are you sure?'

'I'm positive,' said Munro as he drew a breath, 'if he'd slipped because the scaff' was wet with dew, he'd still be warm. Not roasting, perhaps, but warm nonetheless.'

'I never thought of it like that.'

'Well I suggest you start concentrating on the case instead of your boots or you'll not make DS, do I make myself clear?'

'Sir.'

'Have you searched him?'

'Aye. A pat-down.'

'Well, that's something,' said Munro. 'And?'

'Nothing. No phone. No wallet. No keys.'

'And the ambulance service, I assume they were in attendance?'

'Aye, they were,' said Clark. 'They're up at the house if you want a word.'

'And what did they conclude?' said Munro. 'Did they identify any injuries?'

Clark shrugged his shoulders.

'They hardly touched him,' he said. 'They felt for a pulse, checked his chest, and said he was dead.'

'It's reassuring to see the spirit of professionalism is alive and kicking,' said Munro. 'Did they move the body?'

'No. Not an inch.'

'And you, DC Clark, have you completed an inspection of the body?'

'No. I thought that was for the pathologist to do.'

'Give me strength,' said Munro as he held out a hand. 'Gloves.'

Taking his spectacles from his pocket, Munro dropped to his knees and crouched beside the body. Initially perturbed by the lack of bruising, twisted fingers, or even a sprained wrist, his confusion turned to joy as he turned the victim's head to one side and concluded, given the dry conditions and the soft ground, that the ragged gash to the back of his neck, approximately one inch deep and three inches long, was not inflicted as a result of a fall but by an instrument with a serrated blade.

'Right,' he said, as he jumped to his feet. 'That's me away.'

* * *

Munro fastened his safety belt, tossed Murdo a treat, and hit redial on his phone.

'I cannae blame the lad,' he muttered as the call connected, 'we've all got to start somewhere. Och, Mr Byrne. It's James Munro.'

'Again? Are you okay? You're not stuck in traffic, are you?'

'No, no. Listen, ask no questions, but a word to the wise. The gentleman in Raehills Meadows—'

'Are you there?'

'—he didnae fall.'

'What?'

'You've a murder on your hands, Mr Byrne. I suggest you get yourself up here as soon as possible.'

Chapter 7

For artists and romantics alike, the view from the fourth-floor window across the Firth of Clyde to the Isle of Arran was nothing less than inspiring but for Duncan – a bona-fide landlubber whose only experience aboard a CalMac ferry confined him to the men's room as it battled through a stomach-churning gale – the ocean was an unpredictable force of nature best avoided by anyone with an interest in self-preservation.

Turning his back on the deceptively calm seascape he declined the offer of tea and toast, tucked his hands into his pockets, and smiled at the young girl dressed in jeans and a puffa jacket waiting patiently on the sofa.

Life in the modern apartment on South Beach Road for Hannah Cox and her two flatmates would have been ideal were their lives not overshadowed by the actions of their neighbour, a chauvinistic individual who plagued them with complaints about the noise, stole parcels from their doorstep, and bombarded them with lewd comments about the length of their skirts, the shape of their legs and, when rebuffed, their dubious sexuality.

'Is this about the fella next door?' said Cox. 'Has he been moaning about us again? Because if he has, I'm not having it – the man's a creep!'

'Has he been harassing you?'

'Aye! Constantly! He's a lech!'

'Would you like to make a complaint?'

Cox looked at Duncan, dropped her shoulders, and sighed.

'No, you're alright,' she said. 'He'd probably come at us with a chainsaw if he ever found out.'

'Well, it's up to you,' said Duncan. 'Anyway, I'm not here about your neighbour, it's something else.'

'Will it take long? Only I've got work to do.'

'No, as soon as your pal arrives, I'll crack on. What do you do?'

'I'm a courier,' said Cox.

'Really? I have to say, hen, I've not met any female couriers before, do you enjoy it?'

'Aye, it's dead brilliant. I like driving and I like being on my own, so it's ideal. The only downside is having two hundred parcels to deliver. So, why are you here?'

'It's about Freya.'

'She's not back yet. She must have got lucky last night. What's she done?'

'Nothing,' said Duncan. 'Let's wait for your friend, shall we?'

* * *

Sophie Taylor, stick thin with hair as black as jet, padded into the lounge wearing nothing but a bathrobe, caught sight of the rugged stranger standing by the window, and smiled demurely.

'I thought I heard voices,' she said, batting her lashes. 'Who's this, then?'

'Detective Sergeant Reid,' said Cox. 'He's here about Freya.'

Taylor perched on the arm of the sofa, crossed her legs, and brushed her dripping hair from her shoulders.

'Aren't you a bit, you know, rough around the edges for a police?'

'It takes all sorts,' said Duncan. 'Are you comfortable there?'

'Aye. Very. So what's all this about Freya?'

Duncan took a deep breath, held it for a moment, and slowly breathed out.

'I'll not beat around the bush,' he said, softly. 'There's only one way of saying this. Freya's had an accident. A fatal accident.'

The two girls looked at each other and frowned.

'What?' said Taylor. 'You mean, *dead?*'

'Aye. I'm afraid she's not coming back.'

Taylor slipped from the arm of the sofa, sat beside her friend, and took her hand.

'What happened? Was she run over?'

'As much as I'd like to, I'm afraid I can't say anything just now. We have to investigate the circumstances surrounding her death. I hope you understand.'

Respecting the silence that descended on the room, Duncan paused a while before continuing.

'Do you want some time to yourselves?' he said. 'I can come back later, if you like.'

'I'm not sure,' said Taylor as she stood. 'I feel like I'm having a dream.'

'I can arrange for a family liaison officer to come to sit with you. She's trained to deal with situations like this and she'll be able to answer any questions you might have, within reason, of course. Trust me, she'll be a great help.'

'Aye, okay,' said Taylor. 'No. I don't know. Sorry, I need to phone work.'

Taylor left the room leaving Cox looking utterly lost and alone on the couch.

'I know this seems like a stupid question,' said Duncan, 'but are you okay?'

Cox glanced up and glowered as if waking from a nap.

'I'm thinking,' she said, 'about my parcels. Folk'll be fizzing if I don't deliver them today.'

'We can work a way around that. Give me the number and I'll call the depot, another courier can take your load.'

'No. I think I'd rather work. It'll take my mind off it.'

'Is that wise?' said Duncan. 'No offence, hen, but your concentration's not going to be great just now.'

'I'll be fine. Honest.'

'Alright, if you're sure, but let's just wait until the FLO gets here. At least that way your pal won't be left on her own.'

'Aye, okay.'

'Listen. I need to take a look at Freya's room, would that be okay?'

Cox shrugged her shoulders.

'I don't see why not.'

'Good. I don't have a warrant so maybe you'd like to come with me. We could have a wee chat too, if you're up for it.'

* * *

Duncan paused by the door to Freya's room as Cox, looking slightly bewildered, grabbed a pillow from the bed and clutched it to her chest.

'It's immaculate,' he said as he eyed the spotless mirrored wardrobe, the chest of drawers, and the matching bedside tables, 'it's like one of those show homes. When I was your age, I couldn't move for pizza boxes and empty beer bottles.'

'Typical male,' said Cox, mustering a smile. 'If you didn't have a woman to keep you right, you'd all be extinct.'

'Right enough. If it wasn't for my Cathy I'd still be living like a mink. Is it always like this or did Freya tidy for a reason?'

'No, no, Freya's a clean freak,' said Cox. 'She's always hoovering or washing something.'

Duncan took some gloves from his pocket, walked around the bed, and opened the cabinets before turning to Cox with a frown.

'Was Freya planning on moving out?' he said.

'No. Why?'

'There's nothing here. Not even a book or a box of aspirin.'

'There's nothing much of anything anywhere,' said Cox, 'but that's Freya for you. She's not one for possessions. She always says *buy what you need, not what you want.*'

'I know someone who could benefit from that advice,' said Duncan as he rummaged around the wardrobe. 'Was she happy? I mean, was there anything troubling her, like work or money worries, or boyfriends, maybe?'

'Not that I know of,' said Cox. 'Freya's one of those annoying people whose glass is always half-full, and she didn't have time for boyfriends.'

'Oh? Too busy, is that it?'

'No. She just didn't want to get involved with anyone.'

'Enjoying the single life, was she?'

'Aye, to an extent. I think she'd have enjoyed a relationship but she's got what you might call *trust issues.*'

'How so?'

'She never said exactly,' said Cox, 'but I reckon it's to do with her parents. Her da walked out when she was nine years old. I think she's afraid of being let down.'

'Understandable,' said Duncan. 'Nine's an impressionable age. What about pals? Working the pubs, I bet she had hundreds of friends.'

'No,' said Cox. 'She *knew* hundreds of people but as for friends, it was just us. And Jonnie, of course.'

'Jonnie Miller?'

'Aye.'

'Was he not at college with you?'

'He was. He's a grand fella but not many people get him on account of his dyslexia or something, but his heart's in the right place.'

'Were they close?' said Duncan. 'Freya and Jonnie?'

'As close as they could be. Best of pals. Much to Jonnie's disappointment.'

'What makes you say that?'

'He fancied her something rotten. Always has. A case of what they call unrequited love.'

'Poor fella.'

'Aye. He'll be gutted when he hears about this.'

'He already knows,' said Duncan, 'it was Jonnie who gave me your details.'

'Maybe I should go see him. How is he?'

'He's coping,' said Duncan. 'Let's just say he's coping, for now.'

Dropping to his knees, Duncan pulled a large manila envelope from the bottom of the wardrobe, and peeked inside.

'What's that?' said Cox.

'Memories, by the looks of it.'

'Sorry?'

'Photographs,' said Duncan. 'I'm going to hang on to this, okay?'

'Aye, I suppose so.'

'I'll return them in a day or two. Tell me, Hannah, have you any idea where Freya kept her correspondence? You know, like bank statements, for example?'

'Aye,' said Cox. 'In the bin.'

Duncan raised his head and smiled.

'So she really was a clean freak.'

'Freya and clutter, separated at birth. Sometimes she'd not even open the envelope, she'd just toss it straight in the recycle.'

'What about a computer? Does she own a laptop or an iPad?'

'No way. She thought the internet was full of negative energy and the likes of Facebook and the rest of social media made people ill.'

'She might be right.'

'Her phone was as far as she went with technology. She used it for email and banking, but that was about it.'

Duncan stood, tucked the envelope under his arm, and offered Cox a reassuring smile.

'Sounds to me like Freya would've been more at home in the Outer Hebrides. Anything for a quiet life, eh?'

'Aye, pure and simple, that's Freya. Pure and simple.'

'If you remember anything you think might help me,' said Duncan, handing her a card, 'someone she met or didn't like, or if you just need to talk, give me a call. The family liaison officer should be here soon.'

Chapter 8

With life in London a closed book and the memory of her fiancé as faded as a sheet of sun-bleached newsprint, West – at home with the Baltic winters and the kind of scenery that spurred the likes of James Norie, Jacob More, and Alexander Nasmyth to capture Caledonia on canvas – pushed her baker boy cap to the back of her head and huffed in disgust at the images on her laptop as Dougal, narked by the subtle but irritating interruptions, raised his arms in despair.

'What is it, miss?' he said, despondently. 'I'm trying to concentrate here – is it the Thomson girl?'

'It's curtains.'

'For the fella who killed her?'

'No, for me,' said West. 'It's daylight robbery.'

'What is?'

'Ninety quid for a pair of purple tartan blackout curtains.'

'Well, if you buy cheap, you'll buy twice,' said Dougal. 'Have you not got some serious work to do?'

'As it happens,' said West, 'I'm just skimming through McLeod's post-mortem results and Duncan's not going to be happy.'

'I give up. Let's have it.'

'The actual cause of death was exsanguination.'

'So she bled to death.'

'Yup. Not only did that corkscrew sever the external jugular, it went on to pierce the carotid artery, too.'

'That's plenty.'

'The analysis of bloods and fluids revealed nothing unusual, there's no contamination so she wasn't spiked and she wasn't responsible for the puke on the floor of the ladies' toilets either which means some other charming young lady must've chucked up before she got there.'

'Seems to me like that pub attracts quite a classy crowd.'

'Doesn't it just. He's fast-tracked skin and hair samples from beneath her fingernails for DNA profiling and he reckons if there's a match, we should see it on the system in three or four hours. Oh, and the murder weapon's been dusted but there's no prints.'

'Is that it?' said Dougal.

'For now.'

'So it was an out-and-out brutal attack, nothing more?'

'I'd say that's enough, wouldn't you?'

'No, no. What I mean is, there was no evidence of an ulterior motive, of a sexual kind?'

'Apparently not,' said West, 'but as far as a motive's concerned, let's not forget he nicked her bag.'

'Aye, but maybe that was just a consolation prize, after all, he did dump it.'

'True.'

'So why? Why attack her so viciously?'

'That, dear Dougal, is why we are *here* and not behind the till at Sainsbury's. Either way, the question remains, was it a spur of the moment attack, or was it premeditated?'

'You'll have to tune in next week.'

'How are you getting on?'

Dougal slumped in his seat and rapped his fingers on the desk like a driver who'd hit a cul-de-sac.

'Not good,' he said. 'Not good at all.'

'Why, what's up?' said West. 'You were off to a blinding start.'

'Well, for a start the Macallan man's disappeared into thin air. And then there's the paramedics.'

'What about them?'

'I thought we'd be tracing them as witnesses, right? Not as suspects.'

'But something's changed your mind?'

'Aye. The index plates on the ambulance. They're false.'

West closed her computer, leaned forward, and regarded Dougal with the expression of a curious cat bemused by the scratching behind a skirting board.

'Crafty buggers,' she said. 'So, if they're using false number plates then maybe they're in fancy dress, too. Maybe they're not paramedics after all.'

'Aye, that's what I thought,' said Dougal, 'and I have to admit, it would've been a brilliant disguise…'

'But?'

'But there's one minor detail that tips that theory out the window.'

'What's that?'

'We got the results of the bloods on Bewley. He's in good health apart from one thing.'

'I'm listening.'

'Propofol. They found traces of propofol in his system.'

'I've never heard of it.'

'It's an anaesthetic,' said Dougal. 'It's used before a general in major surgery but also for outpatients, but here's the thing; the onset of action is just fifteen to thirty seconds and with a wee dose the effects will only last ten to fifteen minutes.'

'So you're thinking they must be real paramedics to get their hands on the stuff?'

'And to administer it, aye.'

'Okay,' said West, 'that sounds plausible. And you're sure the time-frame of the drug matches the amount of time Bewley was out cold?'

'Aye, and it also explains his inability to recall events in detail.'

'Memory loss?'

'It's a side effect.'

'I could've done with some of that myself a few years ago. So, the bottom line is, we're looking for a couple of skint paramedics and they're using dodgy plates so they don't get caught.'

'I reckon that's about it, aye.'

'Then you've only got one option,' said West. 'Grab your helmet and scoot on up to Crosshouse. HR should be able to identify them.'

'Right you are. What are you up to?'

'I'm thinking of lunch.'

'Are you joking me? You've not long had breakfast.'

'And your point is?'

Dougal stood, zipped his jacket, and smiled.

'No offence, miss, but I'm beginning to think you're bulimic. I mean, how can anyone eat as much as you and stay as thin as a rake.'

'Metabolism,' said West. 'I'm like a racehorse. I burn calories at a rate of knots.'

'I'm not being funny, but a racehorse can cover five furlongs in less than a minute. I can't see you doing that.'

'It's called a metaphor, Dougal. A metaphor.'

'I can think of another word. Right, that's me away.'

'Hold on, young Dougal,' said DCI Elliot as he blustered through the door. 'You might want to hear this.'

The hulking George Elliot, a leviathan of a man known as "The Bear" – a moniker he'd been saddled with ever since his days as a beat officer when the very sight of him was enough to breathe fear into any villain intent on purloining a car or relieving an unsuspecting victim of their hard-earned cash – was firm but fair in his approach to policing and carried only one burden in his otherwise contented life; his wife's dogged determination to see him shed a few pounds by placing him on a largely vegetarian diet which had hitherto done nothing but play havoc with his constitution.

'Will this take long?' said Dougal. 'Only I was just on my way to the hospital.'

'Are you unwell?'

'No. It's to do with the robbery at Bewley's.'

'Then you can wait,' said Elliot. 'There's been a heist. On Newmarket Street.'

West turned to Elliot and proffered a cheeky smile.

'A heist?' she said. 'Are we in Chicago, now?'

'Alright, a hold-up then. Irvine's, the jewellers. Uniform are in attendance but it seems the fellow in the shop was seriously assaulted, you'd do well to get there before the poor chap expires.'

'Well, don't look at me,' said Dougal. 'I've got to get to Crosshouse.'

'My shout then,' said West. 'Let's go.'

Chapter 9

Set away from the hustle and bustle of the high road, Newmarket Street – a tranquil, pedestrianised thoroughfare where folk ambled like tourists in unfamiliar terrain – might have been described as "quintessentially quaint" by many a visitor had the town planners, during its redevelopment, opted to enhance the area by laying cobbles along the lane, erecting period streetlamps, and insisting that any signage be rendered in a traditional style.

Instead, the use of cheap block paving, LED lighting, and garish plastic signs above many a shop drew groans of disappointment from travellers and locals alike.

However, aside from a boutique-style gift shop, an artisan café, and a Grade C listed nineteenth-century pub, one other establishment proud to reflect their heritage was a fourth-generation family business known as Irvine's, an understated yet decidedly upmarket jeweller whose timber façade, topped with an elegant hand-painted sign and an over-sized station clock, regularly drew an audience of window shoppers with little or no desire to remortgage their homes for the sake of a platinum pendant to drape around their necks.

West, having left her Defender parked precariously around the corner, caught the eye of a uniformed constable standing outside the store, his hitherto uneventful day invigorated by the sight of a lissom lady in black jeans and a figure-hugging white tee-shirt strolling towards him.

'Sorry, miss,' he said, 'I'm afraid the shop's closed just now.'

'Just as well,' said West, as she produced her warrant card. 'If it was heaving with customers I wouldn't be able to do my job now, would I?'

* * *

West closed the door behind her and paused as she eyed a strapping young man in a blue-striped shirt sitting on a chair in the corner of the shop, his shoulders hunched and his head bowed like a dejected boxer who'd been pummelled by a formidable opponent whilst a second man, similarly attired, hovered helplessly by his side proffering a mug of hot, sweet tea.

'Mr Irvine?' said West. 'Mr Neil Irvine?'

The confused proprietor looked up without raising his head and nodded.

'And you are?'

'Detective Inspector West. Shouldn't you be in the hospital?'

'I'm not one for hospitals,' said Irvine. 'Besides, there's nothing wrong with me.'

'Are you sure?'

'No bumps. No bruises. No broken bones. I'm fine.'

'I was told you'd been assaulted.'

'I tripped,' said Irvine. 'I must have banged my head when I fell. That's all.'

'Even so, you should get yourself checked out,' said West. 'The last thing you want is an embolism coming back to haunt you.'

'I commend you on your bedside manner.'

'I do my best,' said West, turning to his assistant, 'and you, sir, who might you be?'

'Scott McCallum,' said the young lad. 'I'm his nephew.'

'And you work here, too?'

'I do, aye.'

'And were you both here when the incident took place?'

'We were,' said Irvine, sitting up. 'There's always two of us on the floor at any given time.'

'Good. In that case, do you feel well enough for a chat?'

'No bother,' said Irvine. 'I'll fetch you a chair.'

'You stay where you are,' said West, raising a hand. 'I'll stand. You say there's always two of you in the shop. Is there a reason for that?'

Irvine glanced at West and smiled.

'Look around, Inspector. I'd say that was pretty obvious, wouldn't you? You'd not believe some of the chancers we get in here.'

'Oh, I think I can,' said West. 'Where I come from, if it's not nailed down you can kiss it goodbye. So, as best as you can remember, talk me through what happened, and take your time, there's no rush.'

McCallum placed the mug on the counter, slipped his hands into his pockets, and leaned against the wall.

'Well,' he said, 'it started when a lady came in not long after we'd opened.'

'So it was quiet?'

'Aye. Neil was busy behind the counter changing the till roll on the printer so I stepped up to serve her.'

'What was she looking for?'

'She was interested in the necklaces behind you. Two in particular caught her eye, the Celtic cross in white gold, and the one next to it in silver.'

'What was she like?'

'Very pleasant,' said McCallum, 'attractive in a weathered kind of a way. Late thirties, I'd say. She had blonde hair tied back in a ponytail.'

'And she wasn't bothered about the price?'

'Not at all. She was well-spoken – Edinburgh if I'm not mistaken. Anyway, she couldn't decide between the two so she went to fetch her friend for a second opinion. I had to laugh because she was almost knocked over by another customer coming in.'

'So you served him while she was out?'

'No, no. I did,' said Irvine. 'We had a wee chat. He was a nice fella, clearly minted.'

'How could you tell?' said West.

'I've an eye for these things. He was wearing a Burberry coat over a two-piece suit. Leather shoes, and he wore cufflinks. There's not many folk wear cufflinks these days.'

'And what was he after?'

'A new watch,' said Irvine. 'He showed me the one on his wrist, a Rolex Oyster. He said he'd grown tired of wearing it because it was too heavy. He wanted something just as good but lighter, so I pulled out a selection for him to look at.'

'And what happened next?'

'The lady came back with her friend,' said McCallum. 'She showed him the necklaces and he convinced her to go for the gold.'

'Can you describe him?' said West.

'Nothing special. He was what you might call ordinary. About five-ten, thinning hair, slim build.'

'And what was he wearing?'

'Same as her,' said McCallum. 'Green.'

'Green?'

'Aye. The same uniform. They were paramedics.'

Adopting the kind of expression normally reserved for someone who'd sat on a drawing pin, West, not normally lost for words, stared at the assistant with her mouth agape.

'Are you okay?' he said. 'Only you're not looking too well just now.'

'Déjà vu,' said West. 'I'm experiencing déjà vu. So what happened next? I take it you were both behind the counter?'

'Aye, that's right,' said McCallum. 'I was wrapping the necklace and Neil was having a wee bit of bother fastening a watch on the other fella's wrist when the lady accidentally knocked her bag off the counter.'

'So it fell on the floor?' said West. 'Where? This side?'

'No. Next to me. I bent down to pick it up and next thing I know, Neil's landed on top of me.'

'I'm surprised I didn't flatten him,' said Irvine, 'I'm a heavy lad.'

'Right enough, then I panicked,' said McCallum, 'I mean, he was out cold so I slapped him round the face a couple of times.'

'Hold on,' said West. 'You just fell over? You don't remember being boshed over the head or anything like that?'

'Not at all,' said Irvine. 'I think I would have felt it, if I had.'

'And the paramedics? Did they not help?'

'They did, aye. The lady came round, shoved me out of the way, and bent over him. It looked like she was checking his breathing or something.'

'And then?'

'She didn't look happy. Not happy at all. She grabbed my hands and showed me how to pump his chest then said she had to fetch the defibs from the car.'

'And let me guess,' said West. 'She never came back.'

'No. She did not,' said McCallum. 'Nor did her friend.'

'And the bloke buying the watch, he disappeared too?'

'Aye, he did,' said Irvine. 'And I'm thinking he took the watches with him.'

'Watches?' said West. 'You mean more than one?'

'All four,' said Irvine. 'I'd laid out four for him to look at.'

'Please tell me he was after a Timex.'

'I wish. It was two Omega Speedmasters. They're about nine grand each. A Tag Carrera, two and half grand. And an Oris Aquis, three grand, give or take.'

'I don't think it's a mug of tea you need,' said West, 'I'd get a stiff brandy if I were you. So, that's when you called for an ambulance?'

'Aye, and the police,' said McCallum, 'but by the time they got here, Neil was back on his feet.'

'I still think you should get yourself checked out,' said West, 'and I'd like you to do one thing for me, Mr Irvine, give a blood sample, too.'

'Blood? Why?'

'Because I don't think you tripped. I think the reason you fell over is because you were drugged.'

'Impossible. I didn't take a drink or eat anything.'

'Just trust me on this, okay? I'll get uniform to run you up to the hospital. I've got another officer up there already, he'll take care of you.'

'Aye, okay,' said Irvine. 'If I must.'

'Good, now what about cameras?' said West. 'I'm assuming with a set-up like this, it must be like Fort Knox around here.'

'Aye, cameras aplenty.'

'I'm not up on technology but I need a copy of all the footage surrounding the time of the robbery. How do I get my hands on that?'

'I can do that for you,' said McCallum. 'Are you wanting it now?'

'Yes, please,' said West, 'and while you're doing that, see if you can clock the registration of the paramedics' ambulance for me.'

'No bother. I'll jot it down. Give me five minutes.'

* * *

Recognising the registration as different to the one recorded at the scene of the Bewley robbery, West, well aware that with only a handful of ANPR cameras in the whole of Ayrshire, all of which were on the motorway, anyone using false number plates, especially an ambulance, was unlikely to be caught, instructed the officer on duty outside the shop to run a check on the index while she called Dougal, informing him of Neil Irvine's imminent arrival and the fact that he appeared to have been targeted by the same gang.

The constable, keen to note West's telephone number alongside the vehicle's registration, returned with a cheesy grin on his face.

'The index, miss,' he said smugly, 'it appears to be legit.'

'Back of the net!' said West, excitedly. 'So it belongs to a Honda CR-V, then?'

The officer's smile vanished as he cleared his throat.

'No,' he said, apologetically. 'Not exactly. Sierra, Golf, fifty-nine, Delta, Mike, Charlie, belongs to a 2009 Vauxhall Corsa. Is that not the vehicle you're looking for?'

'No,' said West, bluntly, 'it bleeding well isn't! Have you got the keeper's address?'

'Aye,' said the officer as he tore a sheet of paper from his notebook. 'They're in Kilmarnock. It's a breaker's yard.'

'A breaker's yard? Are you having a laugh?'

'That's what it says.'

'Oh well,' said West, 'this is going to be fun. Right, I need one last favour. Get someone to relieve you, then run the owner up to Crosshouse, as quick as you can. A DC McCrae will be waiting for you.'

Chapter 10

Often referred to as "the queen of hire and fire", the dour and undeniably portly Ms Riley – her ID badge dangling from her neck like a medal from the charisma-bypass championships – looked up from the pages of *Hello!* magazine and pointed to the chair opposite as she wired into a Tunnock's teacake.

'Police?' she said, dusting crumbs from her blouse.

'Detective Sergeant McCrae, madam.'

'It's *Ms*.'

'Sorry. Ms.'

'Sit!'

Unprepared for the matronly manner of the head of human resources, Dougal, as petrified as a pupil about to be castigated for speaking out of turn, duly complied and sat with his helmet in his lap.

'So, you're after some of my staff, are you?'

'Aye. I'm trying to identify two of your paramedics.'

'Why? Have they broken the law?'

'It's possible,' said Dougal, as he slid a couple of print-outs across the desk. 'Let's just say *they're of interest*.'

Riley glanced briefly at the photos and answered succinctly.

'They're not mine,' she said.

'Well, perhaps they're not based here,' said Dougal, 'maybe they're down the way at University Hospital, or Lamlash, even.'

'So, you're wanting me to go through the entire roster of everyone who works for the Ayrshire and Arran Trust?'

'Just the ambulance staff, if you wouldn't mind. I'm sure it won't take long.'

Riley rolled her eyes and huffed as she thumped away at the keyboard.

'Right,' she said, flipping the screen, 'it's like a rogues' gallery. Tell me when you're done and I'll click on the next page.'

Dougal scanned the grid of sixteen passport-style images, each underlined with the name and job title of the employee, before nodding and moving on.

'They're not there,' he said, several pages later. 'Have you no more?'

'None.'

'Okay, then I need to see all members of staff qualified to undertake medical procedures. Can you filter that?'

Riley puffed her cheeks and groaned.

'Here,' she said. 'That's everyone from cardiothoracic surgeons to skin specialists but I'll tell you this, you'll not find them crewing an ambulance.'

Without a match for either of the suspects, Dougal – convinced that only a qualified medic would have the wherewithal to obtain and administer a drug like propofol – dismissed West's suggestion that they might in fact be imposters and, assuming that they'd travelled from the nearby districts of Greater Glasgow and Clyde in the north or Dumfries and Galloway to the south, concluded that the only logical course of action would be to widen his search.

Thanking the frosty-faced Ms Riley for her co-operation, he stood and made for the door.

Whilst a large percentage of those with the ability to recall past events in vivid detail considered it a curse which roused them in the middle of the night as the subconscious mind randomly shuffled distant memories like a fruit machine in a gambling arcade, for Dougal, an eidetic memory was a positive plus in the course of any investigation.

Turning on his heels, he raised an arm and pointed at Riley's computer.

'Sorry,' he said. 'Page two, second row down, third photo from the left. Who's the fella in the purple tie?'

Riley begrudgingly scrolled back through the pages and double-clicked the image.

'This one?' she said. 'He's a locum.'

'Why is he flagged in red when all the others are in blue?'

'It normally means there's a stain on his record,' said Riley as she opened his file. 'Uh-ha. It seems he was the subject of an inquiry late last year. Two alleged cases of negligence where one patient almost died.'

'So, he's been struck off?'

'No,' said Riley. 'Insufficient evidence to sustain the allegations. Apparently there were mitigating circumstances.'

'Which were?'

'Personal. That's all it says.'

'So, he's still working?'

'He's still *allowed* to work, aye.'

'But you've not employed him here?' said Dougal. 'At Crosshouse?'

'No, not since he was suspended pending the results of the inquiry and by the looks of it, neither has anyone else in the AA Trust.'

'That's smashing,' said Dougal, as he handed Riley his card. 'Can you email his details please, I'm needing his full name, address, and phone numbers, and I'll need a copy of that photo, too.'

* * *

Eager to pursue what he believed to be a pertinent line of inquiry, Dougal raced downstairs to find a uniformed officer with a smartly dressed civilian already waiting in the foyer and beckoned them over with a wave of his warrant card.

'Mr Irvine?' he said.

'Aye.'

'DS McCrae. How are you feeling?'

'Not bad,' said Irvine, 'but this is going to raise a few eyebrows, isn't it?'

'What is?'

'Me arriving on the arms of a police officer. Folk'll think I'm some kind of a convict.'

'I'd not worry about that,' said Dougal. 'Right, you need to follow the pink signs to "laboratories", they're expecting you.'

'Is he needing an escort?' said the officer.

'Not necessary,' said Dougal. 'Are you running him back to town?'

'I am. Aye.'

'Then just wait here, he'll not be long. One wee jag and that's him away.'

'Do I not have to wait for the results?' said Irvine.

'No, you're alright,' said Dougal. 'It'll take an hour or two for them to analyse your blood and they'll send the results straight to me. Is there anything else you'd like to ask before I go?'

'Aye, there is,' said Irvine. 'The lady detective who came to the shop, she thinks I may have been drugged.'

'It's a possibility.'

'So, what is it you're looking for exactly?'

'For want of a better word,' said Dougal, 'a sedative. It's harmless enough but it'll knock you out for a minute or two. You're not convinced?'

'No, I am not,' said Irvine. 'I mean, how could they drug me without me knowing?'

'We're working on that. Before you go, can I have a wee peek at your hands?'

Irvine shrugged his shoulders and held his hands aloft as Dougal examined each in turn and sighed.

'Something wrong?' said Irvine.

'No, no. I thought I might find something, that's all. Can you roll your sleeves up for me, please?'

Dougal smiled, reached for his phone, and took a snap of a small, red bump on Irvine's forearm, not unlike a mosquito bite.

'Thanks very much,' he said. 'We'll be in touch.'

Chapter 11

Fortified by a family-size bucket of Southern fried chicken, two corn cobs, and a tub of coleslaw, a rejuvenated Duncan set about sifting through the photographs from Freya Thomson's apartment when West, depriving him of a moment's solitude, burst through the door and snatched the last bag of French fries from his desk.

'Help yourself,' he said, laconically.

'Don't mind if I do. What have you got there?'

'Photos from Thomson's flat. I found them in her wardrobe.'

'Anything interesting?'

'Nothing yet,' said Duncan, 'they're quite old. It looks like they've been pulled from a family album.'

West pointed to a group shot taken in front of an artificial Christmas tree.

'I recognise her,' she said, 'the woman in the middle, that's her mother. No idea who the others are though.'

'I don't suppose it matters,' said Duncan, pushing a print to one side.

'Are you keeping that one for a reason?'

'I'm not sure,' said Duncan, 'there's something about it, the location, maybe. It'll come to me sooner or later.'

'Who is it?'

'That, would you believe, is Freya Thomson.'

'She's a chunky little thing.'

'Aye, you'd not recognise her now,' said Duncan, 'a size six and very pretty, too.'

'A regular ugly duckling, then? You look knackered.'

'Actually, I'm not bad. I feel better now that I've eaten.'

'Even so,' said West, 'I think you should get going. You need to rest. How'd it go with Thomson's mates?'

'As you'd expect. Grief, shock, horror. An FLO's keeping one of them company until the other finishes work.'

'She's gone to work?'

'Aye, she seems to think it'll help her cope, you know, take her mind off things.'

'Did they mention anything about Thomson? Any skeletons in the closet?'

'No. She's as pure as the driven snow,' said Duncan, 'but she strikes me as something of an enigma.'

'In what way?'

'Well, she works in hospitality, she knows hundreds of people, and by all accounts she was a happy wee lass but outside of work she kept herself to herself.'

'Maybe she just liked her privacy,' said West.

'Aye, maybe. Or maybe she was keeping her head down.'

'Why would she do that?'

'I've no idea,' said Duncan, 'but see here, miss, she's not into possessions, her wardrobe's half empty, and she doesn't even own a computer. Maybe my mind's working overtime but I'm finding that just a wee bit odd for a girl her age. I'm thinking she may have been suffering from depression and not even known it.'

'Is it worth following up?'

'I'd say so, aye. I've already contacted her GP to see if she was on any medication or if she even discussed it with him. We'll have to wait and see what he says. How about you? You seem far too happy to have been in the office all day.'

'I haven't,' said West. 'I've been to town.'

'Shopping or lunch?'

'Neither. A robbery.'

'Are you joking me?'

'I kid you not. Some fancy jeweller on Newmarket Street's been relieved of a few watches.'

'Is that all?'

West finished the fries, tossed the bag in the bin, and grinned.

'All told,' she said, 'they're worth about twenty-five grand.'

Duncan leaned back, stretched, and scratched his head.

'In that case,' he said, 'it's fitting that once they've been caught they'll be doing time. Were they armed?'

'That all depends on what you mean by armed. Have a guess at who the likely culprits might be.'

'I've not got the energy for a quiz,' said Duncan. 'Ronnie Biggs? Bonnie and Clyde?'

'Close. It looks like it's the same outfit who robbed the whisky shop. A man and a woman both dressed as paramedics.'

'I know the NHS is underfunded, but there are other ways of supplementing your income. At least tracing an ambulance shouldn't be difficult.'

'You're right, it shouldn't,' said West, 'only I've got a suspicion these two aren't real paramedics.'

'How so?'

'The rapid response vehicle they've been using is carrying false plates.'

'So, we're humped?'

'Not yet,' said West. 'The ones they used on the whisky job were completely made up but we managed to trace the ones they used this morning to an old Corsa.'

'No offence,' said Duncan, 'but you'll not get far with that. Even if you've got the keeper's address all you'll find is a car with no number plates.'

'Not if it's a breaker's yard. Are you busy?'

Duncan returned the photos to the envelope, slipped the one he'd put to one side into his pocket, and cleared the lunch wrappers from the desk.

'Not anymore,' he said. 'I've taken statements from Jonnie Miller and Tam McDonnell, so that's me done. Oh, that reminds me, where's Dougal?'

'He's up at Crosshouse,' said West, 'with the owner of the jewellers. They're getting some bloods analysed. Why?'

'McDonnell's having trouble with his cash register, he says the takings don't tally with the stock and he thinks it might be a software glitch.'

'So what's that got to do with the price of eggs?'

'I told him Dougal would take a swatch at the OS. If anyone can find a fault, he can.'

'Good luck with that,' said West. 'He's flat out and as soon as he gets back I've got the footage from the robbery for him to go through.'

'Well, there's no rush. I reckon McDonnell deserves a break, it won't do us any harm to help him out. Think of it as community policing.'

'Well, if you're free,' said West, 'you can come with me.'

'Where to?'

'I'm going to have a word with the owner of the Corsa.'

'Can you not handle that yourself?' said Duncan. 'Two minutes ago you were telling me to go home.'

'Yeah, I know, but you said you feel fine. Besides, it's a scrapyard, I might need some muscle with me. It's probably full of meatheads carrying crowbars and hammers.'

'They'll not be crushing cars with their bare hands, miss. The fact of the matter is, it's probably run by a couple of skinny neds pushing a few wee buttons.'

'And if it isn't?'

'This is what they call emotional blackmail,' said Duncan. 'Right, let's go, but you're driving.'

* * *

Assuming, somewhat naively, that the journey to the yard would offer the ideal opportunity to sit back and relax, Duncan instead was treated to a twenty-five-minute ordeal akin to a fairground ride during which, aside from bouncing on the rock-hard suspension, he was buffeted by a howling wind blasting through the broken air vents as West, driving like a rookie in a Cowdenbeath stock car rally, hurtled along the A77 in the hope that the sat nav would guide them to their destination.

Lying to the east of Prestwick Airport in a lush, rural location, the breaker's yard, comprising a corrugated-steel grain store, two shipping containers, and a wooden shed which served as an office, languished in an overgrown wilderness which, without the benefit of any signage, ensured a degree of privacy from any prying eyes.

West slowed to a crawl, pulled off the main road, and drove along a dirt track before coming to a halt by the ramshackle shed.

'I've not made many mistakes in my life,' said Duncan, as he stepped from the Defender, 'but asking you to drive was one of them.'

West gave him a nudge, nodded in the direction of a balding, middle-aged man wearing a bunnet and a hi-vis fiddling beneath the bonnet of a doorless car, and swaggered towards him with her hands in her pockets.

'Are you the owner?' she said, disarming him with a smile.

'Aye. Is it parts you're after?'

'No, I'm looking for Stuart. Stuart Keane.'

'You've found him,' said Keane, eyeing the Defender. 'Are you wanting rid of that? Because if you are, I'll happily take it.'

'Do you buy a lot of cars, then?'

'Aye, a fair few.'

'In that case,' said West, 'I was wondering... does it have to be done by the book?'

Keane, interpreting the question as a deal-maker, flashed her a grin and winked.

'Not necessarily,' he said. 'If you want me to take it off your hands, no questions asked, then I can do that for you.'

'I'll bear it in mind,' said West as Duncan sauntered up behind her.

'Have you been doing this long?' he said, glancing at the cars stacked three high in the grain store.

'Twenty years,' said Keane. 'I don't crush them. I strip them and recycle them.'

'It's nice to know you're doing your bit for the environment,' said Duncan, pulling his warrant card from his back pocket. 'You'll not mind showing us your ELV permit, then.'

Keane dropped the smile and, deeming ignorance the best form of defence, hesitated before answering.

'Sorry,' he said with a frown. 'You've got me. ELV?'

'End-of-life vehicle,' said Duncan. 'Every breaker needs one.'

'Oh, *that* ELV. I believe my application's still going through.'

'Twenty years in business and your application's still going through? I'm not buttoned up the back, Mr Keane.'

'Alright, alright. I've just not got around to it.'

'But in the meantime you're buying cars from any ned who turns up on your doorstep?'

'Look,' said Keane, 'I'm just making a living, okay? I *do* strip the cars, and I *do* recycle them, *and* I pay my taxes. I'm not defrauding anyone.'

'I don't doubt that,' said West, 'but without checking where the motors have come from you could be guilty of art and part as far as disposing of stolen vehicles is concerned. There's quite a tasty jail term goes with that.'

'So, is that why you're here?' said Keane. 'To persecute a hard-working member of society?'

'I wouldn't dream of it,' said West. 'We're looking for a Vauxhall Corsa and given what you've just said, I have to say I'm quite surprised that it's legally registered to this address.'

'Then I must have bought it off a law-abiding citizen,' said Keane as he wiped his hands. 'Have you got the registration number?'

'Yup.'

'Then I'll have the details in the office. Follow me.'

West stood to one side as Keane limped by, punched Duncan on the shoulder, and grinned as she pointed to the word "PARAMEDIC" emblazoned across the back of his yellow jacket.

'I'll keep him busy,' she said, softly. 'You call it in, then have a quick mooch around.'

* * *

Turning his back on the setting sun, Duncan – requesting the assistance of a back-up unit – looked across the field and stood transfixed by the stunning plumage of a cock pheasant amongst the tall grass before terminating the call and meandering around the voluminous grain store where, aside from an assortment of vehicles in varying states of disrepair, lay a small packing crate filled with neatly paired bundles of discarded number plates.

Of the two shipping containers, the first – a faded, blue affair with rusted hinges which prevented the doors from closing – was cluttered with several propane gas cylinders, mechanics' mobile tool chests, old oil drums, worn tyres, and racks of salvaged wing mirrors, door handles, headlamps and insignia badges.

Expecting the second to be a dumping ground for any non-recyclable detritus, Duncan opened the doors and sniggered at the sight of a gleaming Honda CR-V in a yellow and green Battenburg livery with a couple of standard-issue responder's backpacks lying by the offside rear wheel, one of which was packed with newspaper whilst the other contained four bottles of whisky.

* * *

'I thought you'd got lost,' said Keane as Duncan wandered into the shed. 'Did you see anything you like?'

'Oh, aye,' said Duncan. 'Plenty. The game's a bogey, pal.'

Keane rang a finger around his collar and coughed.

'I'm not with you,' he said.

'Stuart Keane, I'm arresting you under Section 1 of the Criminal Justice Act on suspicion of assault and robbery, reset, fraud, and ABH. The reason for your arrest is that I suspect you've committed an offence and keeping you in custody is necessary and proportionate for the purposes of bringing you before a court. Do you understand?'

Keane took a handkerchief from his pocket, dabbed his forehead, turned to West, and frowned.

'Listen, I think you've got the wrong fella here, whatever it is you're—'

'Do you understand?'

'Aye.'

'You're not obliged to say anything but anything you do say will be noted and may be used in evidence. Do you understand?'

'Listen,' said Keane, 'this is just one big misunderstanding, I'm sure once you hear me out...'

'I'm not in the habit of repeating of myself, pal,' said Duncan. 'Do you understand?'

'Aye.'

'Good. I need your name, date of birth, place of birth, your nationality and your address. You have the right to have a solicitor informed of your arrest and to have access to a solicitor.'

'Right,' said West, 'grab your coat and leave the hi-vis here. Now, where's your mate? The woman?'

Keane hung his head and took a deep breath.

'She's at home,' he said. 'Probably getting the supper on.'

'Is it far?'

'Tarbolton. Smithfield Crescent.'

'Good,' said West, 'then we'll pick her up on the way.'

Chapter 12

Yet to reach his seventieth birthday, the indefatigable James Munro – unwilling to let a minor inconvenience like triple bypass surgery slow him down – regarded his occupation as a vocation and his duty in life to identify, pursue, and convict the perpetrators of heinous crimes. However, having accepted retirement as a means of safeguarding his health, the subsequent restrictions on his ability to access necessary information, even as a volunteer, was frustrating his attempts at solving his latest conundrum.

Employing the skill, tact, and deceit that only comes with years of experience at the sharp end of murder investigations, coupled with his subliminal ability to think like the most conniving of criminals, he attempted to cajole his ex-colleague, Dr Andy McLeod, into offering some unofficial assistance from the soundproofed security of his car before venturing up to the office.

'Dr McLeod,' he said. 'How are you keeping?'

'Very well, James. To what do I owe the pleasure?'

'Is this a good time or have I caught you on the hop?'

'It's never a good time in the land of the living dead but in your case, I'll make an exception.'

'I'm much obliged,' said Munro. 'Are you keeping busy?'

'As always. Has Charlie not told you about her latest discovery?'

'Not yet. I've just arrived at the office and I'm hoping she's still here. Is it something of interest?'

'I'll not say,' said McLeod, 'it'll only distract you.'

'No bother. Listen, I'm needing a wee favour.'

'I thought you might be. And if it's a wee favour you're after, am I right in assuming it's off the record?'

'Come, come,' said Munro, 'you know I'm a stickler for the rules.'

'Aye. And quite the comedian, too. What do you need?'

'They found a fellow in Raehills Meadows this morning.'

'Raehills? But that's in Dumfries—'

'Your knowledge of the area is exemplary.'

'—and that's not your patch.'

'Quite right,' said Munro, 'but the investigating officer, he's not the sharpest tool in the shed, I feel he might benefit from my somewhat extensive expertise.'

'Oh, aye?'

'They believe the chap in question suffered an accident. A fall from some scaffolding.'

'But?'

'But he has a knife wound to the back of the neck.'

'So you've seen the body?'

'I happened to be passing at the time.'

'Of course you were,' said McLeod. 'So what do you want?'

'They'll be conducting a post-mortem about now. Would you mind having a wee word with your friends in D&G? I'm after a name, an address, and the precise cause of death. You might also like to see if they've recovered the weapon.'

'You're not wanting much, then.'

'I cannae help it,' said Munro. 'I feel duty-bound to help.'

'Have you not got enough feathers in your cap already, James?'

'I'm done with feathers, Dr McLeod, but I'll not rest easy while there's a murderer on the loose.'

'And of course, you can't go through the appropriate channels and request the information yourself?'

'There's a time factor,' said Munro. 'Besides, do you think I'd get far as a volunteer on somebody else's patch?'

'Right you are,' said McLeod. 'Leave it with me, James. I'll give you a wee call as soon as I have some news.'

* * *

Unfazed by the minimalist style of their overnight accommodation, Stuart Keane and his partner, Jennie Ferguson – a remarkably calm individual whose only concern upon her arrest was what to do with the half-cooked pot of stew she'd had simmering on the hob – hunkered down for the night whilst Duncan and West, safe in the knowledge that their quarry could be held for twenty-four hours before being charged or released, headed for the door, their departure delayed by the arrival of a feisty terrier with an ageing detective in tow.

'Jimbo!' said West. 'What are you doing here? We're just about to shove off.'

'Then my timing is perfect,' said Munro. 'I've not stopped all day and I've a raging hunger. What are we having?'

'By which you mean what am I cooking while you cadge a free meal and a bed for the night.'

'I'll buy, you cook, I cannae say fairer than that. Duncan, how are you?'

'Aye, not bad, Chief. Yourself?'

'I'm famished. No offence, laddie, but you're looking somewhat jaded.'

'So would you if you'd not slept for two days. I'm fair fit for my pit.'

'I admire your dedication,' said Munro. 'Sadly it's a quality as rare as hen's teeth amongst some of today's serving officers. Where's young Dougal? Should he not be clocking on if you're clocking off?'

'He's with a robbery victim,' said West, 'getting some bloods analysed.'

Munro regarded West with the subtlest of smiles.

'And why,' he said, 'would the victim of a robbery be needing their blood analysed?'

'You can't stop, can you?' said West. 'Always poking your nose into other people's business! Well, I'm saying nothing, besides, you still haven't said why you're here, what are you up to?'

'Keep your voice down, Charlie! If Elliot gets wind of this he'll not be happy and I'm not in the mood for an ear-grating.'

'So you're at it again,' said West, smiling as she zipped her coat. 'You've been sticking your oar in where it's not wanted.'

'There's a difference between *wanted* and *needed*, lassie.'

'Well you can fill me in over dinner. And as you're buying, I fancy a steak. Fillet. A big one.'

Chapter 13

Unlike a sizeable portion of the working population who, after the trials and tribulations of a twelve-hour shift would opt to kick off their shoes, run a bath, or slouch on the sofa for a moment's respite, West, prioritising sustenance over sleep, slapped the steaks on the hob and uncorked a cheap but perfectly quaffable Côtes du Rhône while Munro, tending to the needs of his best pal above his own, fed a ravenous Murdo before taking a seat at the dining table and raising his glass.

'Your very good health,' he said. 'Is there anything I can do?'

'There is,' said West, as she slipped a tray of chips into the oven. 'You can sit there and drink your wine while I get this ready.'

'Happy to oblige but there's nae rush, Charlie. You need to relax.'

'I will, as soon as I've got this down my neck.'

'No, no. I mean, generally. Are you not socialising much these days?'

'I've no time for that,' said West, as she shed her coat. 'There's too much going on.'

'Well, you should make time,' said Munro. 'All work and no play makes Jack a dull boy. Do you not fancy a wee night out? A few drinks with that nice Dr McLeod, perhaps?'

'Give it a rest. I'm not ready for another relationship.'

'Well there's nae harm in dipping your toe in the water, so to speak.'

'There is with old Redbeard,' said West. 'He might be keen but what he really wants is a wife, a mortgage, and two-point-four, and I'm not doing that. Now change the subject. How's the house coming on?'

'It's coming down nicely.'

'Down?'

'Aye. Just a few wee alterations.'

'I'm not sure I like the sound of that.'

'Trust me,' said Munro, 'when it comes to traditional, I have impeccable taste.'

'I'm sure you have,' said West, 'but that's not what bothers me. It's you ending up back in the hospital.'

'I'm not an invalid, lassie. Not yet.'

'What are you doing exactly?'

'I'm not a fan of plasterboard,' said Munro, 'especially when it's hiding a two-hundred-year-old granite wall, so it's coming off.'

'So you bought this house off the Flintstones?'

'Once it's sealed and had a couple of coats of paint, you'll wonder why it was ever covered in the first place.'

'I'll take your word for it,' said West. 'Do you want some veg with this?'

Munro raised his eyebrows and said nothing.

'That'll be a no, then. So, come on, how come you're so keen to avoid The Bear?'

'I happened across an incident,' said Munro. 'On the Raehills Estate.'

'Where's that?'

'It's not far from Moffat.'

'But that's out of your jurisdiction—'

'You and McLeod have a lot in common.'

'–shouldn't you be leaving it to DI Byrne? You've already helped him out, if he's not up to the job then…'

'I'm not going to denigrate the man in his absence,' said Munro. 'I've given him a pointer or two but I've an urge to keep an eye on the case. It'll not look good for the force if somebody else is murdered.'

'You mean this *incident*'s a body, and the killer's still on the loose?'

'That's precisely what I mean. The SIO's convinced it was an accident. He was adamant the chap had taken a fall from a scaffolding rig. Were it not for my intervention, they'd have left it to the pathologist to find the gaping hole in his neck.'

'Well, have you got anywhere with it yet?'

'I'm making progress,' said Munro as he sipped his wine. 'Dr McLeod's going to have a chat with his friends in D&G so I should have a name by the morning.'

'What was he like?' said West. 'Old? Young? Short? Fat?'

'Young enough. Mid–twenties, fashionably dressed, if you can call a tee-shirt and jeans fashionable these days. Still, at least it was nice to see bovver boots making a comeback. I've not seen them since my youth.'

'Was he a skinhead, then?'

'Quite the opposite,' said Munro, 'he'd have given Rapunzel a run for her money with the mane he was sporting. Right, lassie, it's your turn. If Dougal's out and about during the hours of daylight I can only assume you've a lot going on.'

'I've got more cases than a fire sale at Samsonite, and it's not slowing down.'

Pausing to slide two blackened steaks and a mountain of chips onto the plates, West topped up the glasses and sat opposite Munro whilst an optimistic Murdo watched from the sidelines.

'To start with,' she said, 'two robberies in two days, high-end gear, whisky and watches. The perps are a couple masquerading as paramedics.'

'Some folk have no shame. Have you apprehended them?'

'Yup, we booked them in just before you arrived.'

'How did they manage it?' said Munro as he tore through his steak. 'One would assume a vintage whisky and a watch of value would be kept behind closed doors.'

'They were,' said West, 'but that's the beauty of their get-up! Dressed like paramedics they come across as instantly trustworthy, don't they?'

'Aye, you have a point, Charlie. You do indeed, have a point. But did the victims not chase after them?'

'They would have done,' said West, 'if they hadn't been drugged.'

'Go on.'

'Propofol.'

'Ah! The drug of choice when it comes to sedation. Rapid onset, wears off quickly, and apart from slight memory loss and an upset tummy, nae side effects.'

'Yeah, I know that,' said West, 'but the thing I'm struggling with, is how? Neither of the victims were given anything to eat or drink, so how did they do it?'

Munro closed his cutlery, wiped his mouth with a napkin, and took a large sip of wine.

'Hypodermic syringe,' he said. 'I hear they're all the rage in nightclubs these days.'

'Sorry, Jimbo, am I missing something here? A syringe?'

'Come, come, keep up, lassie, it's easy. A wee jag and that's their victim out for the count.'

'Nah! That can't be right,' said West, 'they'd have felt it!'

'They probably did, Charlie, but they'll not remember it.'

'Wouldn't they need to find a vein?'

'Not necessarily,' said Munro, 'the back of the hand would do, or an arm or leg, any limb you like, it'll not make a difference, nae difference at all.'

'That,' said West, as she cleared the plates, 'is just what I wanted to hear. You, Jimbo, have earned yourself a dram.'

'I dinnae mind if I do. Two fingers, please. Is that it?'

'You mean apart from a young woman getting stabbed in the neck? Yeah, I'd say so.'

'Is she involved in the robbery caper, too?'

'No, this is something completely different,' said West. 'It happened after a disco in a pub. She was a mate of the bloke who organised it.'

'Nae suspect?'

'None, so far,' said West. 'The only real thing we've got to go on is a set of latent prints taken from the scene. They're off a pair of DMs.'

'I was right about the bovver boots, after all.'

'What do you mean?'

'Dr. Martens, Charlie. The original and still the best. And as any discerning yob would tell you, only a twelve-hole in oxblood will do.'

Moving to the comfort of the couch, Munro regarded his phone with the contemptuous look of a disgruntled consumer caught off-guard by a servile member of a customer service team in a call centre five thousand miles away.

'Munro!' he said gruffly, as he answered the phone.

'James. Andy McLeod.'

'By jiminy! Dr McLeod, I do apologise. I'm not wearing my glasses and I couldnae see who was calling. If you're phoning at this time of night I can only assume you have some news or you've been arrested.'

'Sadly, it's the former,' said McLeod. 'I've not got time to break the law even if I wanted to.'

'What have you got?'

'Robert Hines. Twenty-seven years old. Stab wound to the back of the neck. Precise cause of death: severing of the spinal cord between the C1 and C2 vertebrae. The weapon was recovered from the scene, a shallow-tipped hawkbill knife with a serrated 73mm blade.'

'Nae prints?'

'None,' said McLeod. 'Whoever handled it was wearing gloves, and a good job too, it's a razor-sharp piece of kit. Ideal for cutting rope and cable and the like. Incidentally, James, you can rest easy about DCI Elliot, he'll not give you grief for being involved in the case.'

'How so?'

'Are you with Charlie?'

'I am indeed.'

'Then she should hear this, too.'

'I'll pop you on speaker.'

'Alright, Andy?' said West, rolling her eyes. 'I take it this isn't a social call, then?'

'Afraid not, Charlie. Another time, perhaps.'

'Perhaps. So what's up?'

'Are you across the incident at Raehills?'

'Yup, Jimbo's already filled me in.'

'Well, I've some good news,' said McLeod. 'The lads in D&G uploaded the fella's DNA. It's a match to the skin I retrieved from Freya Thomson's fingernails.'

West, lacking the gravitas to accept the findings with the decorum of a senior officer, paused for a moment, drained her glass, and grinned at Munro.

'Get in there!' she said. 'So we've got her killer?'

'I'd say so,' said McLeod, 'unless she had a tussle with somebody else before she was murdered.'

'Blinding! The only downside is he's brown bread, too.'

'At least it'll save on the paperwork.'

'I don't suppose you know what he was wearing on his feet?'

'I've no idea,' said McLeod. 'Would it make a difference?'

'It would seal the deal if they were a size-ten pair of Dr. Martens.'

'I'd have a word with D&G, Charlie, they'll see you right.'

'I cannae thank you enough,' said Munro. 'At least now I have a legitimate reason for pursuing this inquiry.'

'Anytime,' said McLeod. 'I hope you find who it is you're looking for.'

Assuming any serving officer below the rank of Chief Constable should be willing and able to contribute to an on-going investigation regardless of date, time, or circumstance, Munro — unabashed about disturbing one the least competent detectives he'd ever had the misfortune to meet — scrolled through his list of contacts, pressed dial and waved an empty glass at West.

'Charlie,' he said, 'another dram if you would, I've an urgent call to make. DI Byrne? It's James Munro.'

'No offence, Mr Munro, but is it not a bit late to be calling? I'm about to have my supper.'

'Then I apologise, but it'll not take long.'

'Is it important?'

'No, no. Just the wee matter of a murder to deal with.'

'You're talking about Raehills?'

'I am, aye.'

'Well, with all due respect,' said Byrne, 'as much as I appreciate your help, Mr Munro, that's one for us to deal with.'

'Not anymore,' said Munro. 'The fellow in question was responsible for the murder of a young girl here, in Ayrshire, so I believe an appropriate phrase just now would be checkmate.'

Munro smiled at the brief but satisfying pause on the line.

'Right,' said Byrne. 'How can I help?'

'Frankly, I'm not sure you can, but it's worth a try. The deceased, Robert Hines, what do you know about him?'

'He was a casual labourer brought in to help the crew setting up for the festival.'

'The music festival this weekend?'

'Aye. We found his coat beneath the stage he appeared to be working on. That's how we ID'd him, from his wallet.'

'And the weapon?'

'A blade,' said Byrne. 'That came much later, after a hands and knees sweep of the area.'

'And are you any nearer to ascertaining why he was there alone? At night?'

'No,' said Byrne, 'but we did find something in his coat pocket that might or might not be connected.'

'I'm listening.'

'A wee Jiffy bag containing sixty-three pouches of cocaine.'

'Cocaine?' said Munro. 'Are you sure?'

'Aye. Each pouch is a gram. Street value for the whole lot somewhere around two and a half to three grand.'

'And you dinnae regard that as motive enough for his attack?'

'I'm not sure,' said Byrne. 'Aye, maybe.'

'If he was working at Raehills, do you not think he'd have been hiding it there?'

'Maybe.'

'Do you not think that he may have been followed and ambushed for his drugs?'

'Maybe.'

'And that whoever attacked him failed to find the cocaine?'

'Maybe.'

'Jumping Jehoshaphat! You've an awful lot of maybes in your vocabulary, Mr Byrne! I suggest you add some definitelys by the time we next speak or I promise you this, you'll be on your own, Mr Byrne! You'll be on your own!'

West sat back and grinned.

'That told him,' she said. 'I bet he's not got much of an appetite, now!'

'Och, it's all an act,' said Munro. 'Some folk just need a little motivation, that's all.'

'I know. I've still got the bruises. Top-up?'

'Given the circumstance,' said Munro, 'aye. It would be churlish not to.'

West grabbed the Balvenie from the counter, turned to Munro, and froze as she experienced an epiphany.

'Flipping heck,' she said. 'Did you just say festival?'

'At Raehills? Aye, they've a music festival this weekend.'

'I need to call Duncan.'

'He'll not thank you for it.'

'He bleeding well will. That's where Jonnie Miller's playing so he might know the geezer you found dead. In fact, he might even know who killed him.'

Chapter 14

With the equanimity of a cold-blooded assassin and the composure of a Zen master, Duncan – regarded by many as unemotional – rarely raised his voice when threatening a suspect and could barely muster a smile when on the receiving end of an unexpected gift whereas Dougal, as hyper as a deranged Doberman on a diet of dopamine, would explode with joy at the sight of a slice of tiramisu.

Booted from his bed at 4am by his partner, an exhausted Kay Grogan who'd failed to tolerate the glow of his laptop, he'd repaired to the office to continue his research into the efficacy, side effects, and administration of propofol before compiling a comprehensive dossier on the career and lifestyle of Dr Ian Barrie while he waited like a champagne cork preparing to pop for West to arrive.

'Miss! You'll not believe this!' he said as she trudged through the door. 'When I was at Crosshouse trying to trace the para...'

Dougal's words tailed off as West, unable to cope with a full-frontal assault first thing in the morning, raised a finger to her lips, removed her coat, and made a coffee whilst he shuffled anxiously on the spot waiting for his cue to continue.

'Right,' she said, gasping as she swigged her coffee, 'shall we start again or do you need to breathe into a paper bag for a couple of minutes?'

'The Macallan man! I found the Macallan man!'

'Good for you.'

'He's a part of the team that robbed Bewley's and the jewellers! They're all in it together!'

'I'd offer you a coffee,' said West, 'but I think it'll probably do you more harm than good.'

'You're alright,' said Dougal, 'I've got my Irn-Bru.'

'Six of one,' said West. 'Talking of jewellers, did you get the bloods off Irvine?'

'I did, aye. Positive for propofol.'

'Good. Now that we've got that out of the way, we can move on. So, what's all this about the Macallan man?'

'Dr Ian Barrie. Age forty-seven,' said Dougal. 'He's a locum and he's been working with NHS Ayrshire on and off for the last nine years and get this, he's an anaesthetist. That's how come they're using propofol and I think I know how they did it!'

'Let me guess,' said West, 'he used a syringe and gave them a jab in the arm or the back of the hand.'

Dougal, having had the wind taken out of his sails, stood as still as a boat becalmed in the doldrums and stared forlornly at West.

'Aye,' he said, 'but how did you know?'

'Not me,' said West. 'Jimbo cracked it last night. What else have you got on him?'

'He messed up last year,' said Dougal. 'Twice. He was the subject of an inquiry but they concluded it was nothing serious. That said, he's not worked since.'

'Do we know what happened?'

'Aye, the first case was an outpatient; a simple knee operation. Ian Barrie nearly sent him into a coma.'

'Bloody hell,' said West, 'I'd call that serious.'

'The second was in theatre, an appendix removal, same thing.'

'So he was exonerated but he's not worked since?'

'Aye. They say there were mitigating personal circumstances and put his mistakes down to a temporary mental aberration.'

'But hang on,' said West, 'if that's the case, if he was persona non grata, how did he get his hands on the propofol?'

'I'm guessing he stole it,' said Dougal. 'Either before his suspension or after he was cleared. He'd have had free access to the hospital.'

'Well there's one way to find out. Ask him. We've got the paramedics locked up downstairs so we may as well invite this Barrie bloke to the party, too. You know what to do.'

'I'm on my way.'

'Have you got help?' said West. 'I can't see you getting him on the back of your scooter.'

'They're waiting downstairs.'

'Good, give me a shout when you get back, I'll be in the interview room. Oh, and by the way, the two patients he nearly polished off, it's probably not important but do we know who they were?'

Dougal went to his screen and scrolled through a copy of the inquiry.

'Aye,' he said. 'The appendix case was a Mrs Jacqueline Brady and the fella with the dodgy knee was a Mr Stuart Keane.'

Reeling at the mention of Keane's name, West – suddenly finding Dougal's enthusiasm as contagious as the common cold – downed her coffee and frantically scribbled some notes ahead of the interview as Munro, confused by her dawn departure, arrived with Murdo at his heels.

'I remember a time,' he said, 'when we'd need a block and tackle to raise you from your bed. Now you're at your desk and it's not even the back of seven.'

'Sorry, Jimbo, it's like I said, we've got a lot going on.'

'Well, I was under the impression that my overnight stay would be along the lines of a B&B, Charlie. Not self-catering. I'm in need of a brew, are you wanting one?'

'What I want,' said West, 'is some breakfast. I've got a feeling it's going to be a long day.'

* * *

Unlike his superiors who, after a decent supper and a good night's sleep appeared suitably refreshed, Duncan – lumbering into the office with a bulging carrier bag hanging from one arm – looked as though he'd spent a restless night in a musty bivouac on the banks of Loch Doon.

'Dear God,' said Munro, 'you look worse than you did yesterday. Did you not get any sleep?'

'Not much,' said Duncan, 'not after somebody called me about a fella in a field.'

'Sorry about that,' said West, 'I just thought you should know, that's all. Is that food?'

'Aye, it is,' said Duncan, 'and as I missed out yesterday, I'm having first dibs. The three of you can fight amongst yourselves for whatever's left.'

'Two of us,' said West. 'Dougal's not here.'

'Is he still in his pit?'

'Nope, he's on a shout.'

'At this time of day? That's not like him.'

'I know,' said West, 'but he's super-excited. You should've seen him earlier, he nearly wet himself.'

'How so?'

'He's identified the third man, the bloke who's been hanging out with the paramedics.'

Munro turned to West and smiled.

'It's not Harry Lime, by any chance?'

'Who's Harry Lime?'

'He's... he's before your time.'

'Anyway,' said West, 'this bloke, the Macallan man, it turns out he's an anaesthetist and he's the one who drugged the victims and legged it leaving the other two to make off with the gear.'

'Good result,' said Duncan, 'Dougal's not bringing him in alone, is he?'

'No. He's got back-up and it's only over the bridge so he won't be long.'

'Whereabouts?'

'Donnini Court, I think.'

Duncan rummaged through the carrier and frowned pensively at West as he wired into a bacon roll.

'Are you sure?' he said. 'Donnini Court? On South Beach Road?'

'That's the one.'

'Do we have his flat number?'

'Dougal has; it's on his computer, why?'

'Six degrees of separation,' said Duncan as he sat at Dougal's desk. 'Donnini Court is where Freya Thomson and her pals stay. Ian Barrie, is this the fella?'

'Yup.'

'Well, you're not going to believe this, but he's their neighbour and according to them he's not a nice man. Not a nice man at all.'

'I'll warn Dougal,' said West. 'Are you going to help with the interviews once we're done here?'

'Aye, no bother,' said Duncan, 'but I've something I need to do first. After what you told me last night, I'm going to meet Jonnie Miller. If this Robert Hines fella was involved with the festival then he might know him. Chief, are you up to anything this morning?'

'I've a meeting with George,' said Munro, 'about the same fellow, but he'll not be here for a while yet.'

'Good luck with that,' said Duncan. 'No offence, Chief, but once The Bear finds out you've been meddling in another D&G case, he's likely to hit the roof.'

'No, he willnae,' said Munro, 'because if Hines is responsible for the death of Freya Thomson, that makes him fair game as far as we're concerned so George cannae refuse to back me up.'

'Rather you than me,' said Duncan.

'I'm not one to speak ill of the dead,' said Munro, 'but I have to admit, it's a shame he passed away. I'd rather see a dealer behind bars than pushing up daisies.'

'Dealer?'

'Aye. According to DI Byrne he was found in possession of several thousand pounds' worth of cocaine.'

'Either way,' said Duncan, 'he's off the streets, so it's not a bad thing after all. Right, that's me. If anyone hears from Kay, tell her to give me a call, I'm waiting on some results.'

* * *

Gino's café, defying the trend for healthy wholemeal baps, smashed avocados, and katsu curry wraps, specialised in traditional deep-fried fodder for customers in need of a calorie-laden, no-nonsense breakfast guaranteed to narrow the arteries and widen the waistline.

Seated in the corner at a Formica-topped table, Duncan, having ordered two mugs of milky, instant coffee, nodded as a bedraggled Jonnie Miller plodded through the door.

'I'm not used to getting up this early,' he said. 'In fact, I'm not used to breakfast.'

'Then you're in for a treat,' said Duncan. 'What are you having? Toast? A bacon buttie?'

'Are you buying?'

'Aye.'

'Then I'll take a full fry-up, thanks. And another coffee.'

'How are you feeling?' said Duncan. 'Are you okay?'

Miller stared across the table and cradled his mug.

'I've not been sleeping much,' he said. 'You know how it is.'

'Freya?'

'Aye. Is that why we're here?'

Duncan glanced around the café and lowered his voice.

'Do you know a fella called Hines?' he said. 'Robbie Hines?'

'I do. Is he something to do with Freya?'

'Maybe. When was the last time you saw him?'

'Saturday night,' said Miller. 'He was at the Selkie.'

'And you've not seen him since?'

'No.'

'What's his story?'

'Nothing special,' said Miller shrugging his shoulders. 'Same age as me. Clever. A bit of a grafter.'

'What does he do for a living?'

'Sparky.'

'I hear he was helping to set up for the festival on the weekend, is that right?'

'I wouldn't know, but I'd not be surprised if he was. Lighting, that's his thing.'

'What about his personal life?' said Duncan. 'Does he have a girlfriend?'

'Hundreds,' said Miller with a smirk. 'They seem to have a thing for his hair. I can't see the attraction myself, I prefer a short back and sides. He is involved, isn't he? I mean, why else would you be asking all these questions?'

Distracted by the vibration in his pocket, Duncan reached for his phone and stood.

'I need to take this,' he said. 'Enjoy your breakfast, I'll be back in a second.'

* * *

'Alright, hen? How's it going?'

'Sorry,' said Grogan, 'I'd have called yesterday but I was that tired.'

'No bother. Have you something for me?'

'I have, aye. The wee bag belonging to the Thomson girl, I found traces of a Class A.'

'Are you joking me?'

'You sound surprised.'

'I am. See here, Kay, after Mother Teresa, Freya Thomson's the last person I'd have expected to be carrying that crap.'

'Well, she was.'

'What was it exactly? Ecstasy?'

'No, no,' said Grogan. 'Cocaine. To be specific, council.'

'Council? So it was low-grade gear full of fillers?'

'Aye. Purity's about sixty percent. It's been cut with benzocaine. Does that help?'

'Not really, hen. If anything it's made my life a wee bit harder.'

* * *

Jonnie Miller, looking as if he'd had his first square meal in fifteen years, mopped his plate with a slice of bread and smiled as Duncan returned to his seat.

'Thanks very much,' he said. 'I never realised how much I needed that.'

'Have you had enough? You could do with piling on the beef.'

'That's plenty, thanks.'

'Let's go back to your pal, Robert Hines.'

'Not really a pal,' said Miller. 'I just know him.'

'Either way, is he one of your punters?'

Miller looked at Duncan and frowned.

'What do you mean?'

'Oh, come on, Jonnie, I've not got time for this. Is he or is he not one of your punters?'

Miller looked sheepishly into his empty mug.

'Aye, he is. Not a regular but I've sold him some gear now and then.'

'And we're talking weed? Nothing stronger?'

'If he's on anything stronger, Sergeant, he's not getting it from me.'

'So you've not taken a step up the ladder yourself?' said Duncan. 'You're not dealing Es, or snow, or mushrooms or anything like that?'

'Away!' said Miller. 'I'm not that stupid! There's too many bampots out there for me to get involved with gear like that.'

Duncan pulled a tenner from his pocket and slid it across the table.

'Right,' he said, 'that's me away. Incidentally, I'll not be coming to your gig tomorrow after all.'

'How so?'

'Change of circumstances,' said Duncan, 'but see here, Jonnie, that doesn't mean you're off the leash, okay? Play it by the book because if I change my mind and find you've overstepped the mark, I'll not hesitate in bringing you in, do I make myself clear?'

Chapter 15

Deriding Thomas Jefferson's claim that all men, regardless of shape, size, colour, or creed, were created equal, DCI Elliot – a rotund Caucasian with agnostic leanings – believed his genes were responsible for encouraging individuals like himself to consume substantially more calories than his slimmer counterparts in order to maintain what he regarded as an unfair share of the bulk.

Arriving earlier than expected under the pretext of an unusually heavy workload in order to escape his wife's breakfast offering of a bowlful of bird seed laced with red and blue berries, he foraged through the top drawer of his desk, his search for a Mars bar or a caramel wafer curtailed by a curt knock at the door.

'James!' he said. 'Am I glad to see you!'

'Likewise, I'm sure,' said Munro. 'Are you well?'

'As well as can be expected. Given the circumstances.'

'Circumstances?'

'Starvation diet. You've not got one of those Kendal Mint Cakes in your pocket by any chance?'

'I'm afraid not, no.'

'More's the pity. So, what's the story? Have you something on your mind?'

'As a matter of fact, I have,' said Munro. 'It's not important, and it's not critical. I just thought I'd give you a progress report on a particular case. What you might call a distant case.'

'Excellent! Then what say you tell me over lunch?'

'I'd rather do it now.'

'So would I,' said Elliot. 'Come along, grab your coat, I'm feeling peckish.'

'Are you joking me, George? Lunch? At this time of day?'

'Lunch? Brunch? What's the difference? The supermarket down the way does a smashing all-day breakfast and you know me, James, I'm more amenable on a full stomach.'

Preferring to blether over the counter of the local butcher rather than shop for pre-packed items in the charmless environment of a large supermarket, Munro – decrying the well-stocked aisles of factory-produced fodder as the leading cause of ADHD, diabetes, and obesity amongst the younger generation – followed DCI Elliot to the restaurant which, he noted, had more in common with a canteen in a house of correction than a place of culinary expertise.

Idling up to the checkout, he proffered a smile for the dour-looking lady in a white, net hat lingering by the coffee machine.

'Morning,' she said, 'what can I get you?'

'The big breakfast and six rounds of toast,' said Elliot, 'buttered mind, I'm not one for margarine. James, what's it to be?'

'Nothing,' said Munro. 'I've had my breakfast.'

'Well I'll not sit here while you watch me eat, that would be rude. Will you not take an egg, at least?'

Munro sighed as he eyed the sign hanging from the ceiling.

'Aye, okay,' he said. 'I'll take an egg. Poached.'

'Good man.'

'And some bacon. And a tattie scone. And a wee slice of black pudding.'

'That's the ticket!' said Elliot. 'You have to agree, James, a meal is so much more enjoyable when taken in the company of others, wouldn't you say?'

'Not if it's wee Murdo,' said Munro. 'There's nae pleasure to be had in eating your supper with a vulture on your shoulder.'

Elliot tucked a napkin into his collar and whispered across the table.

'I know it's not fancy,' he said, 'but this place offers what you might call *value for money*. It's as cheap as chips.'

'Nae offence, George, but you get what you pay for and judging by the size of your plate, I'd say you're in for a healthy bout of indigestion. Let me know when you reach *amenable* and I'll fill you in.'

'I'm there already,' said Elliot as he devoured his meal. 'In fact you might say, I'm in heaven. So, this case you're so keen to talk about, I'm assuming it's about the fellow they found in Raehills Meadows.'

'Sorry?'

'The chap in Moffat. Robert Hines.'

'By jiminy, George! You've known all along!'

'Aye of course I have.'

'How on earth did you...?'

'I had a call last night,' said Elliot. 'Detective Inspector Byrne. He was after a wee chat.'

'Well, that's that,' said Munro. 'He was wanting to file a complaint, is that it?'

'Quite the contrary, James. Truth be known, he was singing your praises. He sent a file over and as you've not got an official email address, I've printed it off for you. You can read it when we get back.'

'And you've read it yourself, of course?'

'Of course,' said Elliot. 'Robert Hines. He's not from these parts, he hails from Portobello. And he's a record, too.'

'What kind of a record?'

'Possession,' said Elliot. 'He'd already had two warnings but when he was caught a third time he was handed thirty-five hours of community service, and he has a six-month suspended sentence for TDA, too.'

'Was this recently?'

'No, no, a few months back. He's been renting a wee flat in Seafield since last August.'

'Well, he's not been in trouble,' said Munro, 'or we'd have heard of him.'

'You're quite right, James. It appears the young man's been keeping his nose clean ever since he got here.'

'I beg to differ,' said Munro, 'it appears he's still been dealing.'

'There's something else you should know,' said Elliot. 'Along with the drugs, they also retrieved a mobile phone from his coat pocket and listed amongst his contacts is one Freya Thomson.'

'Jumping Jehoshaphat, George! And you've been keeping that to yourself?'

'James, it's not even the back of eight. I couldn't have told you any earlier.'

'Aye, okay,' said Munro, 'but on the back of that, you'll have to excuse me, I need to inform Duncan right away.'

'Hold on,' said Elliot, 'let me finish. It seems Hines and Thomson were involved.'

'Are you serious?'

'Never more so. Unfortunately, as they're both dead, we cannot prove it but I'm not aware of anyone in a platonic relationship who'd sign an email with "love you lots" and pop a wee kiss at the end.'

Munro, perplexed as to why Robert Hines, if besotted with Thomson, would choose to kill her, pushed his plate to one side and stared at Elliot.

'Have we any idea how long they'd been seeing each other?'

'There's a clue or two in the transcript of his texts and emails,' said Elliot, 'but all I can tell you just now is that the email I mention was sent the day she was murdered. They'd arranged to meet at The Bonnie Selkie.'

'I cannae thank you enough,' said Munro, 'but right now, I really do have to find Duncan.'

'I'll come with you,' said Elliot. 'We can stop at the pharmacy counter on the way out. I think I need some Gaviscon.'

Chapter 16

Were it not for his callused hands – the only visible consequence of working without gloves in blisteringly cold temperatures – the wiry Stuart Keane could have been mistaken for a post office clerk, an accountant, or a sales assistant in the bedding department of a large department store.

Enjoying a modest lifestyle with his partner of twenty-three years and unable to secure a mortgage as a result of his cash-rich business and fictitious tax returns, Keane's only vice was the lottery which he played with the regularity of a metronome in the hope of winning enough to purchase his own home.

Seated behind an empty desk in the stark surroundings of the interview room, he raised his head, nodded, and smiled politely as West closed the door.

'Morning,' she said. 'Did you sleep alright?'

'Aye, not bad,' said Keane. 'Is Jennie not joining us?'

'I'm afraid not,' said West. 'I'll have a chat with your missus later, it's just the way we do things around here. Can I get you a drink? Tea, coffee, water?'

'No, you're alright, I'm fine.'

'Good, then we'll crack on, shall we? Just a word to the wise, Mr Keane, I've got a shedload of people I need to talk to so I'm not in the mood for any shenanigans. If you don't want to answer a question just say "no comment", okay?'

'I'm not looking for trouble,' said Keane. 'I'll tell you what you need to know.'

'Blinding,' said West as she activated the voice recorder. 'The time is 7:38am. I am Detective Inspector West. Would you state your name please?'

'Stuart John Keane.'

'And for the benefit of the tape can you confirm that you've waived your right to a solicitor?'

'I have.'

'And do you understand why you're here, Mr Keane?'

'Aye. I've been arrested on suspicion of assault and robbery, fraud, and ABH.'

'Very good!'

'But I'm not guilty. Apart from the robbery bit. I admit that.'

'It's not for me to decide whether you're guilty or not,' said West. 'We'll leave that to the courts, shall we? Right, let's start at the beginning: do you admit to the theft of several high-value bottles of whisky, namely a Glenfarclas, an Ardbeg, a Lagavulin, and a Bowmore, worth in excess of thirty-five thousand pounds from Bewley's World of Whisky in Troon?'

'I do, aye.'

'And do you admit to absconding with two Omega wristwatches, a Tag Carrera, and an Oris with a value in excess of twenty-three thousand pounds from Irvine's the jewellers of Newmarket Street in the town centre?'

'I do, aye.'

'Excellent,' said West. 'Job done. I wish all my clients were as honest as you. Right, let's get some flesh on the bones. Do you have any money worries, Mr Keane? Are you struggling or suffering any kind of financial hardship?'

'No, no. I'm not a millionaire,' said Keane, 'but we're not hard-up. We have a modest lifestyle but I'm not ashamed to say I'd not mind being a bit more comfortable, you know, not having to worry about bills and the like, do you understand?'

'I do indeed,' said West, 'but tell me, you're obviously not a habitual criminal so why did you choose to go on a crime spree and rob these establishments?'

'I didn't. What I mean is it wasn't my idea.'

'Would you care to explain?'

'Gladly. I was approached by a fella I'd met before. He asked if I'd be interested in making a few quid by way of recompense for his actions.'

'What kind of actions?'

'If I was being vindictive,' said Keane, 'I'd say attempted manslaughter, but it wasn't. Not really. It was a simple mistake and I'm not one to bear grudges.'

'Hold on just a minute,' said West, 'you'll have to be more specific than that, attempted manslaughter's a serious allegation.'

'The fella was an anaesthetist. Barrie's his name. Dr Ian Barrie. I was in for keyhole surgery on my knee, it's been giving me gip for years. It was only after the operation that I discovered he'd nearly put me under for good.'

'When was this?'

'Last year.'

'And he contacted you out of the blue?'

'He did, aye. He said he felt guilty about what he'd done and wanted to make amends. He said he'd a plan that wasn't strictly above the law but was guaranteed to make us a few thousand each.'

'Didn't it strike you as odd,' said West, 'that a specialist doctor on a hundred grand a year was inviting you to take part in an organised robbery?'

Keane looked blankly at West and shrugged his shoulders.

'I never gave it a second thought,' he said. 'It never even crossed my mind.'

'But as someone who buys stolen cars for a living you were up for it?'

'That sounds a bit harsh,' said Keane, 'but aye, that's the nub of it. I only agreed because it seemed like a foolproof plan. I'm not a clever man, Inspector, but it sounded like a work of genius to me.'

'So what was the plan?'

'He said we'd—'

West raised a hand and stared at Keane.

'Hold on,' she said, '*we*?'

'Aye. Jennie and me. Barrie knew I had a wife, common law, I'll give you that, but a wife all the same, and he said for the plan to work it needed two people to work together. Two people who trusted each other.'

'Okay.'

'He said we'd not need balaclavas or ski masks. If we dressed as paramedics then everyone would trust us.'

'If that's the case,' said West, 'then why not dress as police officers?'

'Because you can be done for impersonating a police officer, but there's no law against dressing like a paramedic or a firefighter. Like I said, he'd thought it through.'

'So how did it work?'

'The plan was he'd go into the shops first, get them to bring all the valuables out, then he'd leave, that was our cue to go in and distract the staff. Then he'd come back, give them a wee drop of something to knock them out, then we'd take the gear out in our bags.'

'Like you say,' said West, 'genius. Weren't you worried?'

'About the drug bit, aye, I was, but he assured us that the stuff he used was harmless and that there'd be no rerun of what he did to me but…'

'But what?'

Keane hung his head and sighed.

'But when I saw the old fella hit the floor in the whisky shop I changed my mind. I wanted out.'

'Why?'

'Listen,' said Keane, 'I know I've not done things by the book but what I do doesn't hurt anyone else. It doesn't affect their health, or their business, or their livelihood. I'm not out to destroy people's lives. That's not me. That's not me at all.'

West leaned back and folded her arms as she pondered the bigger picture.

'I'm a bit baffled,' she said. 'Why go to all this trouble for a few measly grand? I mean, let's face it, even if you and Barrie went 50/50 it's not exactly going to set you up for life, is it?'

'We'd not finished,' said Keane, 'the whisky and the watches was just the beginning. Next on the list was another jeweller in Kilmarnock, a mobile phone shop in the retail park, and a computer shop on River Street, one after the other before anyone could catch up with us.'

'But we did.'

'Aye. And I'm glad of that. Really, I am.'

'So once you'd nicked the stuff,' said West, 'what happened then?'

'He was going to come and collect it but you arrived before him.'

'And the rapid response vehicle? Where'd that come from?'

'I've no idea,' said Keane. 'It was ex-service and it definitely looked the part but it didn't function as it should. The blues and twos had been decommissioned and the medical gear had been stripped out.'

'Did he bring it to you?'

'No, no. I had to collect it from an address on South Harbour Street. He gave me a specific time and said the keys would be in the ignition.'

'And the uniforms?'

'On the back seat.'

'Have you seen or heard from Barrie since the last robbery?'

'The last time I saw him was at the jewellers. He said he'd be in touch about collecting the goods.'

'He obviously trusts you,' said West. 'I mean, what's to stop you making off with the stolen items yourself?'

'Good question,' said Keane with a smile. 'I'd never thought of that.'

'And your wife, Jennie? What did she make of all this?'

'I don't think she realised how serious it was. To her, it was just a game, a wee bit of dressing up and some acting. She'll not be happy now but she enjoyed it at the time.'

'Let's talk about Barrie,' said West. 'Did he give you any options about getting involved?'

'I'm not sure I understand the question?'

'Did he give you a chance to back out? Or did he coerce you, threaten you, even?'

Keane furrowed his brow as he contemplated his answer.

'Not as such,' he said. 'He said if he told us his plan then we'd be obliged to take part. I'd not say he was threatening, menacing perhaps. I suppose he thought if he told us his plan before we agreed then we could tell the police what he was up to.'

'But the bottom line is, you didn't refuse, did you?'

'Unfortunately, no. Mind you, he'll not be happy once he finds out we've been arrested.'

'I wouldn't worry about that,' said West. 'We've nicked him too. Give it a few days and you'll be able to wave at each other across the exercise yard. Right, I'm going to charge you now but before I do I must caution you that you do not need to say anything in answer to the charge but anything you do say will be noted and may be used in evidence. Do you understand?'

'Aye.'

'The charge against you is that you did knowingly steal goods to the value of approximately fifty-eight thousand pounds from two separate establishments in collaboration with two accomplices in the knowledge that their actions may have endangered the lives of your victims. Do you understand?'

'Aye.'

'Have you anything to say?'

'I'd like to see Jennie, if that's possible; just to reassure her. She didn't really take the stuff, it was me, she was just along for the ride. She doesn't deserve to hang.'

Chapter 17

With the strike rate of a professional ten-pin bowler, failure, be it an occasional blip on an otherwise faultless record, was not something Dougal McCrae took lightly.

Sitting with the look of a wean whose guileless guinea pig had been plucked from the garden by a gluttonous goshawk, the dejected detective stared forlornly at West as he contemplated their next move, his directionless thoughts interrupted as Duncan slammed the door.

'Bloody hell,' said West, 'with a face like that you're going to fit in a treat round here. What's up?'

'My head's mince,' said Duncan. 'Freya Thomson. She had traces of low-grade coke in her handbag and I can't figure out why.'

'Maybe she was a closet user.'

'I'm being serious. The girl lived like a nun, it's just not her thing.'

'Well, it looks like Robert Hines is the bloke who topped her and he was done for possession so there's a connection there.'

'I get what you're saying,' said Duncan, 'but even if he was after it, even if he was desperate enough to kill her for it, the question remains how did he know she had it?'

Munro, in the throws of feeding his perpetually hungry terrier, looked up at Duncan and smiled.

'That's an easy one,' he said. 'It seems Robert Hines and the Thomson girl were in a relationship.'

Duncan stared back, cocked his head, and frowned.

'No offence, Chief, but where'd you get that from?'

'DI Byrne.'

'A reliable source then.'

'Och, I know the man's a balloon but I've just come from a meeting with George. They found Hines's phone and there's plenty of texts and emails to substantiate the claim.'

'Why did we not find them on Thomson's phone, then?'

'I've not tried retrieving the deleted messages yet,' said Dougal, 'I've not had time.'

Munro stood and pointed to the desk.

'There's a full report of D&G's progress to date,' he said. 'It's all in there.'

'We'll not get any answers in that,' said Duncan. 'Think about it, if they were an item then surely that's even less of a reason to kill her.'

'That,' said Munro, 'all depends on how stable their relationship was and whether it was one-sided or more business than pleasure.'

'How do you mean?'

'If the drugs did belong to Hines, then perhaps you should consider that fact that she may have been acting as his mule. Or perhaps she stole it from him.'

'No, no. Sorry, Chief, but that's not Freya Thomson. There's something else going on here. I can feel it.'

'You need to give yourself a break,' said West, 'do something to take your mind off things and come back afresh.'

'Aye, you're right,' said Duncan. 'What did you have in mind? Two weeks in Torremolinos?'

'I was thinking half an hour in the interview room.'

'Go on.'

'Dr Ian Barrie. He's only got two words in his vocabulary: "no" and "comment".'

'So that's why you're all looking so miserable.'

'He's not budging,' said Dougal. 'See here, Duncan, we know he's behind the robberies and his accomplices have just given evidence against him but he's saying nothing.'

'Well he's exercising his legal right to remain silent. If you've got the evidence, why not just charge the clown and get it over with?'

'I'm not doing that,' said West. 'I'm not running the risk of him getting off because it all turns into one man's word against another's. We need an admission and you need to let off steam.'

'Sorry, miss, but just what, exactly, do you expect me to do?'

'Just have a chat,' said West. 'Let's face it, the way you look is enough to put the fear of God up anybody. He's stewing downstairs.'

'Aye, okay,' said Duncan, 'but there's one condition.'

'Name it.'

'We go see McDonnell at the Selkie afterwards.'

'Any danger of somebody telling me why?' said Dougal.

'He's got a software glitch on his fancy till. I said you'd take a wee look and sort it for him.'

'Do I have "IT department" stamped on my forehead?'

'You'll have a footprint if you're not careful. Right, that's me, I'll see you in half an hour. Oh, and while I'm gone, do me a favour. Have a word with Thomson's flatmates and see if they've heard of Robert Hines.'

* * *

Though impeccably dressed in a collar and tie with his hair neatly groomed and his shoes shiny enough to catch a reflection, Dr Ian Barrie, still clad in his three-quarter length camel-coloured coat, looked more like a second-hand car salesman than an educated man of means.

Sitting with his hands clasped on the desk and staring dead ahead, he barely flinched as Duncan, declining to acknowledge the suspect, leaned across the desk and stabbed the voice recorder before walking to the back of the room where he stood, hands in pockets, out of Barrie's line of sight.

'DS Reid,' he said gruffly. 'It's 9:57am. State your name, please.'

'Ian Barrie.'

'Are you sure you're not wanting a solicitor?'

'No comment.'

'Do you understand why you've been arrested?'

'No comment.'

'Would you not like to defend yourself against the allegations before you?'

'No comment.'

'Right, well I'm not going to waste my time,' said Duncan. 'I've not slept in three days and I need some rest so we'll cut to the chase. You're here on suspicion of orchestrating a string of robberies, to all intents and purposes, armed robberies, but I'm not bothered about that. Robberies are ten a penny. Murder's more my thing. Let's talk about murder.'

Barrie twitched his shoulders and coughed.

'You've a nice pad in Donnini Court, haven't you?' said Duncan. 'And I'm guessing there's no mortgage to pay on it, after all, you must be earning what, a hundred thousand a year? A hundred and twenty? You've got a fancy Rolex on your wrist and I bet you drive a Jag, or a Lexus, am I right?'

'No comment.'

'The thing is, Dr Barrie, you've not been earning for a while now, have you? And I reckon the whole experience, being the subject of an inquiry and watching your savings dry up, must have been incredibly frustrating. Am I right, Dr Barrie? Was it frustrating? Did it not make you angry?'

'No comment.'

'If it was me,' said Duncan, 'I'd be raging. I mean, how did you deal with that? How did you deal with being accused of negligent behaviour? How did you vent your anger? Did you take a wee drink or two? Did you punch the walls? Or did you take it out on your neighbours?'

'No comment.'

'The three girls who live next door to you. They're young, bright, full of life. They've done nothing to upset you but you instigated a campaign of harassment against them. You intimidated them. Your lewd behaviour left them fearful of opening the front door. Have you any idea how that must have felt?'

'No comment.'

'The sad thing is, one of those girls is now dead. The sad thing is, she didn't die of natural causes. She wasn't hit by a truck. She was murdered.'

Duncan pushed himself off the wall, walked around the desk, and pulled up a chair.

'So that's my line of inquiry,' he said, as he glared across the table. 'Murder. And I think you had something to do with it.'

Barrie averted his eyes and swallowed hard.

'No comment.'

'See here, Dr Barrie, I reckon murder would come easy to you. I mean, you're clearly not that emotional and you've had a couple of practice runs, have you not? After all, you've nearly killed two folk in your care already. Stuart Keane and Jacqueline Brady.'

Duncan, sensing the result he sought was finally in sight, allowed himself a wry smile as Barrie, erupting like Vesuvius, slammed the table with a clenched fist.

'I've not killed anyone!' he said. 'No-one! Ever!'

Duncan, remaining as cool as the proverbial cucumber, scratched his cheek and sneered.

'I don't believe you,' he said, his voice barely more than a whisper. 'See here, Dr Barrie, do you know what upsets me? It's the fact that if you get done for a couple of robberies you'll probably be out in five years. That's the way the system works. Unfortunately. But do you know what makes me happy? It's the fact that if you're convicted of murder, then you'll be looking at life and that will come with a recommendation that you serve a minimum of twenty-five years. Now, that puts a smile on my face. That's why I'm going to prove you're guilty.'

Barrie widened his eyes and glared at Duncan as the veins in his temples swelled and throbbed to the beat of his pulse.

'For the last time, I've not killed anyone!' he said. 'I'm innocent!'

'That's what they all say, until we slap them in the face with the evidence. Where were you last Saturday night?'

'What?'

'Where were you?'

'At home.'

'Doing what?'

'Telly. I was watching the telly.'

'Can anyone verify that?'

'No, of course not! I was alone.'

'Dear, dear, that's you humped then,' said Duncan. 'See, I think I know what you did last Saturday night. I think you had a couple of drinks. Then, I think you went for a walk. I think you followed Freya Thomson to her place of work. I think you waited until she'd finished her shift. Then I think you murdered her.'

'I did no such thing! I had nothing to do with it!'

'But you had everything to do with the two robberies, didn't you? It's your call, Dr Barrie. Out in five, or in for life.'

Believing Duncan to be cut from the same cloth as the bent coppers who occasionally graced the front pages of the national press accused of falsifying evidence in order to secure a conviction, Barrie, caught between a rock and a hard place, panicked and jumped at the softer option.

'Aye, okay!' he said, as he crumbled in his seat. 'Okay. I planned the robberies but I didn't kill anyone. I robbed a couple of shops, that's all!'

Duncan slipped his hands into his jacket pockets, leaned back in his chair, and watched as Barrie dabbed his forehead with a monogrammed handkerchief.

'Right,' he said, 'let's have it, from the top. Apart from yourself, who else was involved?'

'Mr Keane. Stuart Keane, and his wife.'

'Why them?'

'We'd chatted before his operation,' said Barrie. 'He told me briefly about his business and offered me a cash deal if ever I needed a car. I knew he was the type.'

'Is that why you jagged him with too much juice?'

'No. That was a genuine accident. He came to mind after I was acquitted of any wrongdoing.'

'Why did you do it?'

'Why do you think?' said Barrie. 'I was broke.'

'You don't know the meaning of the word,' said Duncan. 'You have no idea what it means to be broke.'

'Maybe not, but I'm used to a certain lifestyle. I have standards to maintain.'

'But no morals. No code of ethics.'

'We each do things our own way.'

'You're not wrong there, pal. You're not wrong there. Did it not cross your mind to get a loan to tide you over? Or to sign on and claim some unemployment benefit, or was that below you?'

Barrie glanced at Duncan and smiled.

'Obviously it is,' said Duncan. 'Well, you know what they say about pride coming before a fall. Let's talk about the ambulance. Where'd you get it? Was it stolen?'

'No,' said Barrie. 'I bought it. All above board. A company on the internet specialising in ex-service vehicles.'

'How did you pay for it?'

136

'Credit card. Five thousand, two hundred, and fifty pounds.'

'And the uniforms?'

'Online. It's not difficult. It's just workwear.'

'And the stuff you nicked,' said Duncan, 'where was that going?'

'Friends. I had several friends lined up who were keen to get their hands on a bargain.'

'Wealthy friends?'

'Well-off friends, aye.'

Duncan checked his watch, stretched, and covered his mouth as he stifled a yawn.

'Drugs,' he said. 'That's your thing, isn't it?'

'I'm an anaesthetist so, aye, in manner of speaking, it is.'

'So how did you get your hands on the propofol?'

Barrie flinched as if receiving an electric shock.

'Propofol?' he said. 'How... how do you know about the propofol?'

'We're not stupid, Dr Barrie. If we can find your DNA in a strand of hair, tracing a drug's a walk in the park. So, where'd it come from?'

'Crosshouse.'

'Did you steal it?'

'Aye.'

'When?'

'When I was cleared of any wrongdoing.'

'And you stole it because you'd already planned the robberies?'

'Aye, like I said, I was getting desperate. I needed the money.'

'Right, that'll do for me,' said Duncan. 'I've things to do so I'll leave you in peace but I'm going to charge you before I go. You do not have to say anything in answer to the charge but anything you do say will be noted and may be used in evidence. The charges against you are robbery and assault, fraud, and ABH. Do you understand?'

'Aye. I understand.'

'Have you anything to say?'

'No,' said Barrie. 'Nothing that'll make a difference.'

* * *

Like a mob of meerkats aroused by the presence of a predator, Dougal, West, and Munro raised their heads in unison as Duncan traipsed through the door.

'Well,' said West, tentatively, 'how'd it go?'

'All done,' said Duncan. 'He's been charged.'

'What?'

'He told me everything.'

'How in God's name did you get him to do that?'

'I wound him up,' said Duncan. 'I said I was going to charge him with the murder of Freya Thomson.'

'But he had nothing to do with it.'

'I know. That's why he opted for the lesser of the two charges.'

Munro shook his head and smiled.

'You're a devious sort,' he said. 'Like a chip off the old block. You'll go far, laddie. Mark my words, you'll go far.'

'The only place I'm going, Chief, is the Selkie. Dougal, grab your coat. You can buy me lunch on the way.'

Chapter 18

Thankful for the fact that he wasn't one of the grey-faced office workers ambling aimlessly past the shops in search of something exciting to alleviate the boredom of their desk-bound jobs during their sixty-minute lunch break, Dougal – toying with a Filet-O-Fish – gazed silently through the windscreen as Duncan polished off the second of three double cheeseburgers and stuffed the wrapper in the glove box.

'You're awful quiet,' he said as he rummaged through the bag for a portion of greasy fries. 'Is there something on your mind, pal?'

'Not really,' said Dougal. 'I was just wondering how you managed to get a confession out of Barrie. I wish I could've done that but you must be better than me when it comes to grilling suspects.'

'You're talking like a dafty,' said Duncan. 'You're just as good, you've just a different way of doing things, that's all. See here, I bet if we went for a walk in the wilderness you'd have a wee map and a compass, and waterproofs, and a packed lunch. Am I right?'

'Aye, of course! Would you not?'

'No. Not me,' said Duncan. 'I'd follow my nose but here's the thing, we'd both get where we were going, the only difference is you'd get there all warm and dry and looking like a professional hillwalker whereas I'd get there soaking wet and chilled to the bone looking like a numpty on day release. Do you get what I'm saying?'

'Aye, you're right,' said Dougal. 'Thanks for that.'

'Besides, you're better at other stuff. McDonnell's till for example. I'd not have a scooby where to start but for you, it's easy. We're not so much chalk and cheese, pal, more neeps and tatties. Right, we'd best make a move or Westy will be wondering where we've got to.'

* * *

Despite the unexpected death of Freya Thomson, the ensuing investigation, and the less than pleasant task of scrubbing, sterilising, and disinfecting the washroom, Tam McDonnell – replenishing the fridges with ridiculously named craft ales, soft drinks, and Mexican beer – was nonetheless looking forward to another cracking Saturday night which, if as successful as the last, would almost certainly save him from closure.

'Mr McDonnell,' said Duncan. 'You alright?'

'Aye, not bad, Sergeant. And yourself?'

'Same as always. This is DS McCrae, half man, half computer. He's here to have a swatch at your dodgy till.'

'I'm much obliged,' said McDonnell. 'Come away around the bar and I'll switch it on for you.'

'I understand you've a discrepancy between what your till's showing and your stock levels,' said Dougal. 'Is that right?'

'Aye, spot on.'

'And you think the till's not registering the sales as it should?'

'Well, I'm no expert,' said McDonnell, 'but it's the only thing I can think of.'

'Well, let's have a couple of dry runs and see what happens.'

Duncan leaned on the bar like a loner in a western and eyed the bottles of fancy bourbon lining the wall.

'What kind of discrepancies are we talking about?' he said. 'Is it a few G&Ts or a couple of bottles of wine?'

'I wish it were,' said McDonnell, 'but it's more than that and it's across the board. Don't get me wrong, I'm not complaining about the amount of money we made, but it should have been more.'

'Can you give us some detail?'

'Aye. I keep six kegs for the beers on tap. Three in reserve and three on the go. I'm on my reserves already and they're down to less than half. Then there's the spirits, mainly white rum and whisky, and I'm down a few other bottles here and there.'

'So what's the damage, roughly speaking?'

'Well,' said McDonnell, 'the kegs are about a hundred pounds each, add in the spirits, and I'd hazard a guess of around fifteen hundred pounds.'

'And you're sure the stock didn't walk out the door?'

'If it was just the spirits, then you might have a point, but it's not possible with the beers on tap.'

* * *

Dougal, stabbing the touch-screen with the speed and accuracy of a bantamweight in a whack-a-mole tournament, stood away from the till and sighed.

'There's no problem here,' he said, 'the till's working fine.'

'Then I don't understand,' said McDonnell. 'It doesn't make sense, no sense at all.'

'Did the folk working the till know what they were doing?'

'Aye. It was the young girl. She had years of experience.'

'So there's no chance she could have been ringing up, say, a bottle of Coke instead of a pint of beer?'

'No.'

'You're sure?'

'Aye. I think so.'

'We could check,' said Dougal. 'Have you any cameras about the place?'

'Only one,' said McDonnell, pointing to the ceiling, 'it's just above your head.'

'How do we get the footage?'

'It's on my laptop. I'll fetch it for you.'

Dougal looked at Duncan, shrugged his shoulders, and apologised.

'Sorry,' he said, 'but everything seems fine. What do you think?'

'I'm thinking,' said Duncan, 'I could go a pint just now. It's been a while.'

McDonnell returned and placed his laptop on the bar.

'Here we are,' he said. 'Just press play. You can fast-forward too if you want to.'

'Aye, I think I'll get the hang of it,' said Dougal as he sped through the recording.

'Can you not claim on your insurance?' said Duncan. 'I mean, can you not file it as damaged stock or something?'

'No chance,' said McDonnell. 'If it were that easy every landlord in the country would be claiming twice a week.'

'Fair point.'

'Right, there's your problem right there,' said Dougal, pointing at the screen. 'It's your second till.'

'Second till?'

'Aye, right there, under bar. It's not wired up to anything. The cash is going in but the sales aren't being recorded. That's why you've a shortfall.'

McDonnell turned to Duncan and frowned.

'But I've not got a second till,' he said. 'That's not mine.'

Duncan glanced at Dougal and nodded towards the door.

'I know what's going on,' he said. 'I'll be back soon, Mr McDonnell, and don't you worry, you'll get your money back.'

* * *

Duncan parked on the shady side of the street, glanced up at the top floor flat, and reached for his phone.

'Dougal,' he said, as he left the car, 'you wait here, I'll not be long. Jonnie, it's DS Reid. I need a word, pal.'

'Where are you?'

'Outside. Buzz me in.'

Scaling the stairs two at a time, Duncan, barely out of breath, entered the tiny flat and gently closed the door behind him.

'Something up?' said Miller. 'You're not looking too happy.'

'I'm not happy, Jonnie. I'm fizzing.'

'How so?'

'Because in all the time I've known you, I've given you plenty of breaks. I've cut enough slack for you to go bungee jumping off the Empire State Building. I've defended you when others were ready to lock you up. But I'll not be taken for a fool.'

'I'm not with you,' said Miller. 'You're talking in riddles.'

'Last Saturday. The gig at the Selkie. You earned yourself a few quid, right?'

'Aye, right. I earned it.'

'Then why did you have to fleece the fella for more? The second till. Start talking or I'll do you here and now on suspicion of theft. Then I'll come back with a warrant and rip this place apart and if I'm right, I'll not only find the cash, I'll find your stash, so I'll do you for possession, too. So, what's the story?'

Miller sat cross-legged on the bed and hung his head.

'I did it for Freya,' he said. 'It was all for her.'

'For Christ's sake, Jonnie, don't go bringing a dead girl into this. I thought you were better than it.'

'I am! It's true! I did it for her. Just hear me out.'

'The clock's ticking, pal. And I'm on a meter.'

'We were in it together. Freya and me. But I've not taken a penny of that cash, it was all for her.'

'Why?'

'She deserved it. After the life she'd had, she deserved it.'

'So you're telling me you're some kind of modern-day Robin Hood? Is that it?'

'No,' said Miller. 'What I'm telling you is that Tam McDonnell is Freya's dad.'

'What?'

'The same dad who walked out on her when she was just a wean. The same dad who left her with a mistrust of men. The same dad who left her scared of relationships.'

Duncan reached into his jacket pocket and pulled out the photo of Freya he'd kept from her rag-tag collection of snaps.

'Now I see it,' he said, as he held the picture aloft. 'That's him, isn't it? That's him and Freya.'

'Aye, that's them.'

'I knew there was something familiar about this. It's been driving me nuts.'

'Well, now you know.'

'But why?' said Duncan. 'Why steal the cash?'

'Because she never had any. She and her mum never had two pennies to rub together. It was a way of getting back at him. Next time we'd have taken him to the cleaners.'

'Did she not want to talk to him? Catch up with him? Find out why he left?'

'At first, aye. But what happened that night changed her mind. Being there, right under his nose, changed her mind.'

'In what way?'

'You hear about these folk,' said Miller, 'families who've been separated for years but when they finally meet again, without being introduced, they recognise each other, but there was nothing there. I saw them lock eyes before he went for his supper, but there was nothing, no recognition at all.'

'How did you know it was him?'

'I tracked him down. It took a wee while because I'm not great at computers but I did it in the end. I'm not as stupid as I look.'

'Go on.'

'He was working in Leith, some big shot in an advertising agency. I went there a few times, sat outside, and just watched him living the high life and swanning around without a care in the world.'

'And how did you discover he'd moved down here?'

'The last time I went he wasn't about. It was the wrong time of the year for him to be on his holidays so I just asked at reception. They said he'd retired and moved to Ayr to open a pub. So I just wandered around until I found him.'

'You missed your calling,' said Duncan, 'you should've been a cop. Either way, I can't condone what you've done, Jonnie. An eye for an eye isn't the way to do things.'

'So you're arresting me?'

'No. I am not. But your freedom comes with two conditions.'

'Name them.'

'First of all, you give me the cash you stole from McDonnell and I'll make sure he gets it back. No questions asked.'

'Aye, okay, fair enough. What's the second condition?'

'You go back to the Selkie and do your gig on Saturday night as promised, and you make it a good one. Got that?'

'Aye. Deal.'

'Good. And, Jonnie, you've no lives left now. Mess up again and you're going away for good.'

* * *

Despite his frustration at being left out of the loop, Dougal, befuddled by his partner's unexplained actions, held his tongue as Duncan slipped into the driver's seat and flicked the ignition.

'Hold this,' he said as he handed him a plastic carrier bag.

'What is it?'

'McDonnell's missing cash.'

'Are you going to tell me what's going on, or are you keeping it to yourself?'

'The second till,' said Duncan. 'It belongs to Jonnie Miller. He and Freya Thomson were in it together. They were out to fleece McDonnell for as much as they could.'

'Is that why you're so annoyed?'

'I'm not annoyed,' said Duncan, 'I'm raging with myself for getting Thomson so wrong. She's what you might call a bit of a dark horse.'

'I don't get it,' said Dougal. 'Did Miller not earn a good whack from that gig?'

'He did, aye.'

'And Thomson must've been paid, or rather, would have been paid for her shift, so why did they do it?'

'If I told you, you'd not believe me.'

'I might.'

'Get this,' said Duncan. 'Tam McDonnell is Freya Thomson's da.'

'Away! Are you joking me?'

'Miller's been on his tail for years itching for retribution. He wanted payback for him walking out on Freya when she just a kid.'

'This might sound odd,' said Dougal, 'but I find that quite comforting. I wonder if she knew just how much Miller liked her.'

'He never liked her,' said Duncan. 'He loved her, but the poor fella was on a hiding to nothing.'

'I've got to hand it to you,' said Dougal as he fastened his safety belt. 'You're on fire today. You should go without sleep more often.'

Chapter 19

Like a long-distance runner driven by an obsessive desire to carry his aching limbs across the finishing line, Duncan – on the verge of collapsing with the tape in sight – shuffled into the office with the shoogly gait of a jakey on a Buckfast binge and slumped into a chair as a lowly Dougal, still berating himself for failing to secure a confession, scooted to his desk and buried his head in his computer.

'At last,' said West. 'I was about to send out a search party. How was McDonnell? Did you fix his till?'

'It wasn't broken,' said Dougal.

'No,' said Duncan, 'but my faith in humanity is.'

'Do you need a spell on the couch or are you feeling sane enough to tell me what's up?'

'Jonnie Miller,' said Duncan, irately. 'He was being economical with the truth, and that's putting it mildly, and as for that Freya Thomson, I should've known better.'

'Dear God,' said Munro, 'it's not therapy you're needing, it's a trip to Dignitas.'

'Thanks, Chief. Ignore me, I'm pure shattered.'

'I'm not surprised,' said West. 'You need to bugger off and get some sleep. I promise I won't ring you tonight.'

'Well, if you do, you'll not get an answer.'

'But before you go, what's all this about Miller and Thomson?'

'They were running a scam together. The plan was to relieve Tam McDonnell of all his hard-earned cash.'

'Why?'

'Because,' said Duncan, 'McDonnell is Freya Thomson's father. It was Jonnie Miller's idea of revenge. He wanted to get back at McDonnell for walking out on Freya and her mum all those years ago.'

'Flipping heck,' said West. 'Well, I have to admit, I didn't see that coming.'

'No, nor did I,' said Duncan. 'But I'm telling you this, Miller's not getting an inch from now on. If he slips up again, I'm hauling him in.'

'Well, I won't stand in your way,' said West. 'I've always thought he was a bad egg. Right, it's time we all knocked off. Dougal, what are you doing?'

'I'm going to crack on with the reports for the fiscal, miss. I'll start with Barrie and take it from there.'

'Don't be silly, you can do that tomorrow.'

'No, no. I'd rather start now. It's the least I can do after this morning's failure.'

'Don't beat yourself up,' said West. 'You didn't fail. Anyway, won't Kay be wondering where you are?'

'No, she's still at the breaker's yard. I may as well keep going until she's done.'

'Well, don't stay late. Duncan, you look like death warmed up. Push off.'

'Roger that, miss. Chief, are you hanging about or is that you back to Auchencairn?'

'I'll be back tomorrow,' said Munro. 'I fear there's a few loose ends need tying up.'

'Loose ends? It's like a bowl of spaghetti.'

'Speaking of which,' said West, 'Jimbo, I've got a bottle of Chianti that needs opening, do you a fancy a pizza? I could order now and we could pick it up on the way back?'

'Aye, why not?' said Munro. 'I'll take a margherita. A large one. Thin crust.'

'Isn't that a bit plain?'

'It's as a pizza should be.'

'Are you sure you don't want some toppings? Some pepperoni or garlic?'

'Certainly not.'

'Anchovies? Peppers?'

'No, thank you.'

'Olives? Mushrooms? Barbecue sauce?'

Munro hooked Murdo to his leash, stood, and glared at West.

'I'm after a pizza,' he said, 'not gastroenteritis.'

* * *

Having dined in some of Scotland's finest Italian restaurants where he'd enjoyed an authentic array of some of the simplest dishes Bel Paese had to offer, Munro – whose knowledge of takeaways was limited to fish suppers – stared at the mountain of minced beef, shredded chicken, and spicy meatballs piled atop West's gargantuan pizza and declared the abomination an insult to Neapolitan cuisine.

'I hope you've a cast-iron constitution,' he said. 'You're going to need it.'

'You don't know what you're missing.'

'I know exactly what I'm missing,' said Munro. 'Should they not have served that in a trough?'

West raised her glass and smiled.

'Maybe they should,' she said, 'because right now I'm as happy as a pig in clover.'

'Touché,' said Munro. 'Touché. Is there anything for dessert?'

'Yup. Cinnamon swirl or a Balvenie.'

'I'll take the Balvenie,' said Munro. 'I'm not keen on bark. So, if young Dougal's busying himself with the paperwork, I take it the two robberies you were dealing with are a done deal?'

'Pretty much,' said West. 'The bloke posing as a paramedic with his wife came clean straight away. He was out of his depth. And thanks to Duncan, the jag-happy doctor finally fessed up to being the brains behind the scheme.'

'I'm not surprised,' said Munro, 'the fellow has a knack of instilling fear in folk, he's like an army dentist extracting a wisdom tooth.'

'You're not wrong there. To be honest, Jimbo, I think Dr Barrie took one look at me and Dougal and thought we were a soft touch.'

'And were you?'

'Not particularly,' said West, 'but he clung on to his right to remain silent. That's why I sent in the heavy mob. The thing I like about Duncan is he doesn't lose his rag, he doesn't go in all guns blazing, he does things quietly like one of those nutters in *Reservoir Dogs*.'

'He's one of a kind,' said Munro, 'I'll give you that, but it's not just his presence, it's the way he thinks. Even if the front door's open, he'll try and get in around the back.'

'Either way, he has put a dent in Dougal's ego, that's for sure.'

'I'd not worry about Dougal. The lad's got more brains than a butcher on market day. So, where does that leave you?'

'Freya Thomson,' said West as she topped up their glasses. 'Or should I say, the mysterious case of who killed her killer and why.'

'I cannae see why you're bothering with that,' said Munro. 'Should you not be leaving that to DI Byrne to sort out?'

'Maybe, but the fact that Robert Hines murdered Freya Thomson has got me hooked. Besides, if I wait for Byrne to get on the case I'll be drawing my pension before he comes up with any answers. Have you got any ideas?'

'Och, Charlie, you should know by now that as a volunteer, I can only advise.'

'That's all I want. Advice. So I'm thinking...'

'Just a moment,' said Munro, 'if you're thinking I need to take my glass and retire to the sofa. Right, on you go.'

'We know Hines and Thomson were having a fling and we know there were traces of cocaine in Thomson's bag so if she was carrying, then we can also assume it was Hines who stole it from her. We also know that, for whatever reason, it was Hines who killed her. The question is: who killed Hines and why?'

'Well, the easy one,' said Munro, 'is the "why". The cocaine, obviously.'

'Yes, but I want the "who".'

'Someone from his past perhaps. He's a history of possession and TDA, with a record like that he's bound to have been mixing with all manner of miscreants.'

'So, D&G haven't identified anyone yet who might've been after him? Anyone who might've known he'd swiped the coke off Thomson?'

'I'm not the SIO, Charlie. You'll have to ask DI Byrne.'

'I'm not doing that,' said West. 'I'll bleeding well work it out for myself if it kills me.'

'What are you wanting? Burial or cremation?'

West smiled as she reached for the Balvenie, filled two tumblers, and returned to her seat.

'I can't believe it's taken them this long to come with this,' she said, flicking through the investigation report. 'There's nothing to it. Have you read it?'

'I have,' said Munro. 'Several times. Over and over.'

'Why?'

'Because I was looking for something that isn't there.'

'Here we go.'

'They recovered a weapon from the scene, did they not?'

'Yeah, a knife,' said West. 'To be precise, a hawkbill knife.'

'And?'

'And nothing,' said West. 'The perp was wearing gloves, so no fingerprints. They tested the bloods, they're a positive match for Hines, and the blade matches the wound perfectly.'

'So what's missing?'

'Apart from a passport photo, a name, and an address, nothing.'

'Think again, lassie. Good grief, Charlie! A DNA test! There's nae mention of a DNA test!'

West sat back, sipped her whisky, and proffered Munro a curious gaze.

'Would that be necessary?' she said.

'By jiminy, Charlie, every stone has to be turned! Every single one! As Dr McLeod pointed out, that knife was razor sharp. That being the case, if there was a struggle between Hines and his assailant, then there's every chance the perp could have nicked himself during the assault.'

'Cut himself? Through a pair of gloves?'

'Charlie. Did it not cross your mind he may have been wearing latex gloves?'

'Flip.'

'So it's not beyond the realms of possibility that the blade itself is carrying two strands of DNA. If I were you, lassie, I'd be putting in a call to DI Byrne and I'd be demanding to know why they've not run a test—'

'You're unbelievable,' said West. 'You're like a blind man who can see in the dark.'

'—and if he's not got an answer, I'd request the weapon be sent to Dr McLeod as soon as possible.'

'Why not send it up to Glasgow. Maybe Kay could take it.'

'Because McLeod is based here so it'll be a damned sight quicker, Charlie. You've not got time to hang around, you're forgetting, there's a murderer on the loose.'

'Well, it's a start,' said West. 'I'm not being ungrateful but I do wish we had more to go on.'

'You have,' said Munro. 'You're just not looking hard enough. I think it's time we had a wee quiz.'

'Oh, not now, Jimbo. I'm tired and I'm not in the mood.'

'Your starter for ten.'

'Gawd, here we go.'

'If I said "possession", what would you say?'

'Drugs, easy.'

'And if I said "TDA", what would you say?'

'Nicking a motor. Taking and driving away.'

'And if I said "ringer"?'

'A stolen vehicle. A stolen vehicle with a fake identification number and false documentation.'

'Well done!' said Munro. 'Maximum points. Now, if you'll excuse me, I'm away to my bed.'

'Hold on, just a minute! What do you mean *bed*? Is that it?'

'That's plenty,' said Munro. 'Read the report from D&G. Read it twice. And sleep on it. It'll all make sense in the morning.'

Chapter 20

Bemused by the widespread belief that Scotland suffered more rainfall in a week than the beleaguered countries of the Indian subcontinent during a wet monsoon, Duncan – who'd burned more times on the streets of Ayr than a sunbathing Brit on the beaches of Benidorm – basked in the glow of the early morning sun as he ambled from the car intent on unearthing the reason behind Freya Thomson's uncharacteristic desire to conceal a consignment of low-grade cocaine in her handbag.

Revitalised by a homemade macaroni pie, two cold beers, and ten hours' uninterrupted sleep, he strolled into the office and, expecting the rest of the team to be hot on his heels, was somewhat surprised to find Dougal already tapping away at his keyboard and a frustrated West, head in hands, glued to the case report from DI Byrne.

'I've heard of early birds,' he said, 'but you two must be suffering with insomnia. Have you been here long?'

'Not long,' said West. 'Half an hour, maybe.'

'How so?'

'Reports to file. Criminals to catch.'

'Is that supposed to make me feel guilty?'

'You,' said Dougal, 'are the last person to feel guilty about anything. Did you not bring any breakfast?'

Duncan reached into his pockets, produced three bacon baps, and tossed one over.

'One for you,' he said, 'one for you, miss, and one for the Chief. What are you reading?'

'The report on Hines,' said West.

'Still trying to figure out who nailed him?'

'Yes, and it's doing my nut in. Jimbo's seen something in this and I can't find it.'

'What you mean is, he's seen something that's not actually written down.'

'Precisely. He started talking about Hines and his record, you know, possession and TDA, then went off on a tangent and started gabbing on about ringing cars.'

Duncan pulled up a chair, swung his feet onto the desk, and stared at West.

'I can see your problem,' he said. 'The three of those don't seem to go together. What did he say, exactly? About the ringers?'

'Nothing. He asked me what a ringer was so I told him. It's a motor with a fake VIN and fake documentation.'

Dougal stopped typing and peered over his screen.

'I'm not being pedantic,' he said, 'but apart from what you've mentioned, a ringer's actually a stolen car using the identity of one that's been written off.'

Duncan looked at Dougal and smiled.

'You're genius, pal. An utter genius.'

'I think you're confusing me with someone else.'

'No, no. See here, if I know the Chief, I reckon he's talking about the breaker's yard.'

'I'm intrigued,' said West. 'Go on.'

'The rapid response vehicle,' said Duncan, 'that was using false plates, and you yourself heard Keane admit to buying and selling stolen vehicles.'

'So you're thinking he might have bought a couple off Hines?'

'Aye.'

'Do you know what? I think you might be right.'

'I hope so,' said Duncan as Munro entered the office. 'I hate cases that drag on and on. Chief, you're late.'

'I've been for a walk with the dog.'

'I'll not blame you for that, it's a cracking day out there.'

'It'll not last,' said Munro. 'This country has more seasons than a Vivaldi concerto. Dreich by dark, trust me.'

West stood abruptly and grabbed her phone.

'Jimbo,' she said, 'you get on with DI Byrne, don't you?'

'Well, he's not on my Christmas card list but, aye, I suppose I do.'

'Do me favour then, would you? Give him a bell and request that knife, I want it asap. Don't take it personally but I've got to go.'

'Where to?'

'I need to speak with Stuart Keane. Urgently.'

Munro glanced at Duncan and winked as she left the room.

'I take it the penny dropped?'

'Like Little Boy on Hiroshima. Are you stopping?'

'I am indeed,' said Munro. 'Breakfast and the newspaper while Murdo takes a nap. And you?'

'I'm going to swing by The Bonnie Selkie. I want a wee blether with McDonnell to check he's okay. With a bit of luck I might even get an idea about Freya Thomson's dealing habits while I'm there. The thing is, Chief, now that we know McDonnell is Freya's da, do I tell him?'

'Tell him what?'

'That the girl murdered in his pub was his daughter?'

'Does he not know?'

'No. He hasn't a clue.'

'That's not an easy one,' said Munro. 'Is he down as a next of kin?'

'He's not down as anything.'

'Then you've no obligation to say anything. What other options do you have?'

'Well, I could wait for his ex to contact him,' said Duncan, 'but they might not even be speaking anymore. Or I could let him find out for himself, he's bound to read it in the paper or see it on the telly in a day or two.'

'If you wait that long,' said Dougal, 'he might go mental because you never mentioned it.'

'Aye, I get that, but I'm worried about tipping him over the edge. Just when he thought he'd turned a corner, he lost a fistful of cash and some valuable stock, plus he's been on the receiving end of an investigation. I'm just not sure how he'll handle hearing about Freya.'

'Then you've a choice,' said Munro, 'between the devil and the deep, blue sea. I suggest you play it by ear, laddie. I'm sure you'll make the right decision.'

* * *

Had he been sitting on the front porch of a timber-clad house in the suburbs of Mobile, Alabama, the pony-tailed Tam McDonnell – hiding behind his tinted shades with a steaming mug of coffee in one hand and a roll-up in the other – might have looked right at home, however, plagued by pedestrians side-stepping his chair on the pavement outside the pub on Alloway Street, his appearance was more akin to a blind beggar than a music-loving denizen of the Deep South.

Duncan stepped from the Audi, crossed the street, and smiled as he approached.

'Alright for some,' he said. 'I see you're rushed off your feet.'

'It's been non-stop,' said McDonnell. 'Will I fetch you a cup? I've just made a pot.'

'No, you're alright, I just stopped by to see how you were doing.'

'I'm not bad. The stock's been ordered and the toilets smell like a hospital ward but apart from that, I'm back in the swing.'

'I'm glad to hear it,' said Duncan as he propped himself against the wall. 'And are you sleeping okay? You're not having nightmares or anything like that?'

'I'm sleeping fine,' said McDonnell. 'Don't get me wrong, I'm not wanting to make light of the situation but I've seen worse things on the television.'

'Aye, right enough.'

'And thanks again for returning the cash.'

'No bother.'

'Where on earth did you find it?'

'It's not important. You've got it back, enough said.'

'Right you are.'

'So, are things okay? I mean, after everything that's gone on, you're not having regrets about moving here, are you?'

'None at all,' said McDonnell. 'It's good to be home.'

'Home?'

'Aye. I was born here. Holmston, near the cemetery.'

'I never realised. So you're not missing Leith?'

McDonnell flipped his Zippo and lit a cigarette.

'Like a hole in the head.'

'Oh?'

'I had nothing there,' McDonnell, 'apart from work. At least here I've a sense of belonging.'

'Is that all you've got? I'm not prying but do you not have any family here?'

'None. There used to be someone but that was years ago.'

'So you don't see each other anymore?'

'No.'

'I take it that means you're not one for digging up the past, then?'

McDonnell drew on his fag and blew the smoke towards an empty sky.

'To be honest,' he said, 'it would be like looking up an old school friend then wishing you hadn't bothered.'

'How so?'

'We were young, Sergeant. Too young. We were in lust.'

'That's not a bad thing.'

'It is when the end result is a bairn you hadn't planned.'

'I see,' said Duncan, 'but would you not want to see him? Or her?'

'Even if I did, it'd not be fair, messing with her head like that, me popping up out of the blue then disappearing again. No, no. That wouldn't be right. Not right at all, Besides, her mother would probably skelp me if she ever saw me again.'

Duncan raised a smile and laughed.

'Sounds like it was daggers at dawn.'

'To be fair,' said McDonnell, 'it wasn't as bad as that, just a classic case of both of us wanting different things.'

'In what way?'

'I wanted to get on with my career and she wanted to see the back of me, so the end result was spot on.'

'Well, I am glad you can laugh about it now. So, if you're all cleaned up, you must be raring to go.'

'Aye, let's just hope I can pull a few punters through the door.'

'Away! I'm sure they'll be coming in droves,' said Duncan, 'besides, I've a feeling Saturday night's going to be a belter.'

'That's where you're wrong,' said McDonnell. 'There is no Saturday night. Not in the way you mean.'

'I'm not with you.'

'He's cancelled.'

'Jonnie Miller?'

'Aye. He rang last night. He said he could do next Saturday but this weekend he's fully booked. He said he's got a gig near Moffat.'

'Has he indeed?'

'Aye. It's a big festival, apparently.'

Duncan checked his watch and pulled his car key from his pocket.

'Well unfortunately for Miller,' he said, 'I think he's going to miss that one, too.'

'What do you mean?'

'Nothing to worry about, Mr McDonnell. I'll leave you to it.'

* * *

Like a simmering kettle about to boil, Duncan flipped the ignition and called the office.

'Dougal,' he said, 'I'm on my way to Miller's place, I need a car to meet me there—'

'No bother.'

'—and a warrant.'

'You'll not get that in time.'

'I know, but I'm not fussed, just get the ball rolling.'

'What's going on? Are you alright?'

'Aye, top of the world. I'll be back in an hour.'

* * *

Used to running the gauntlet of verbal abuse and aggressive behaviour from intoxicated clubbers threatening to rearrange his features if he didn't play the tracks they'd requested, Jonnie Miller was not one to be easily intimidated but the unsettling silence and Duncan's unwavering gaze was enough to have him twitching like a turkey in December.

'Twice in two days,' he said, nervously. 'I should give you my key.'

'That's not a bad idea,' said Duncan, softly. 'You'll not be needing it for a while.'

Miller glanced away and did his best to smile.

'Why's that?' he said. 'Are you buying me breakfast again?'

'No chance,' said Duncan. 'I tend to lose my appetite when folk let me down. It's rude, it's disappointing, and it shows a lack of respect. Call me old-fashioned but that's just the way I am.'

'I'm sorry to hear it,' said Miller, facetiously. 'Who's let you down?'

'I've just come from seeing Tam McDonnell. He says you've cancelled his gig on Saturday night.'

'Aye, I had to,' said Miller. 'I've the festival this weekend.'

'We had a deal. You gave me your word.'

'Sorry, but I'm not cancelling two all-dayers for one night in a pub.'

'So, you're not changing your mind? You've no desire to make amends for what you've done?'

'I have,' said Miller, 'but not just now. Sorry, Sergeant, but I'm doing the festival and you can't stop me.'

Duncan looked to the ground, smiled, and shook his head as he reached behind him and pulled a pair speedcuffs from his belt.

'That's where you're wrong,' he said. 'Jonathan Miller, I'm arresting you—'

'Are you joking me?'

'—under Section 1 of the Criminal Justice Act on suspicion of possession with intent to supply, and theft. You're not obliged to say anything but anything you do say will be noted and may be used in evidence. You know the rest. Get your coat.'

* * *

With a dazed Miller safely on his way to the custody suite, Duncan snatched two plastic sacks from the boot of his car, returned to the cramped flat, and scoured the open-plan quarters for anywhere discreet enough to hide a small-time dealer's stash of weed and amphetamines. However, with little more than a clothes rail and the drawers beneath the divan to look at, he turned his attention to the tiny kitchen where, in the absence of any retaining screws, he lifted a wonky shelf from the base of the unit under the sink to find a brown, cardboard box emblazoned with the logo of an online retailer and a biscuit tin with a faded festive scene printed on the lid.

Prising it open, he grinned as he estimated the bundles of ten and twenty pound notes to be enough to wallpaper the small room whilst the box, aside from layers of clear, resealable pouches not much larger than a matchbox, contained a bulging, plastic bag stuffed with enough council to send a street full of schemies into orbit for a week.

Chapter 21

Unfazed by the less than satisfying outcome of her meeting with Dr Ian Barrie, West – who had a history of breaking down some of the hardest criminals by adopting the persona of a menopausal woman with an undiagnosed bipolar disorder – returned to the interview room with her confidence intact and a ploy to unleash her softer side on an unsuspecting Stuart Keane.

However, unlike the anaesthetist whose stubborn disposition did nothing but delay an inevitable outcome, the wiser Keane, aware that his co-operation might result in a comparatively lenient sentence, was eager to assist the inquiry by answering any questions as best he could.

West, smiling as she entered the room, closed the door behind her and placed a plastic cup of coffee on the table in front of him.

'Two sugars,' she said. 'Is that enough?'

'Spot on,' said Keane. 'Thanks very much.'

'You're welcome,' said West, as she settled into her seat. 'How are you feeling? Are you ready for your big day in court?'

'As ready as I'll ever be.'

'You've not got much to look forward to, have you? I mean, a few years inside, it's not going to be easy.'

'You reap what you sow,' said Keane. 'I've no-one to blame but myself.'

Bewildered by his insouciant if not fatalistic attitude, West leaned back, crossed her arms, and regarded him with a furrowed brow.

'I'm not sure who you remind me of,' she said. 'A parish priest or John Christie.'

'Sorry,' said Keane. 'Christie?'

'He was a serial killer.'

'But I've not killed anyone.'

'I'm not saying you did. I'm talking about your demeanour. Christie was a bit like you; meek, humble even. Softly spoken, mild-mannered and polite, like butter wouldn't melt but all the time, there he was, knocking off people like it was going out of fashion.'

Keane raised his eyebrows and lingered over a sip of coffee.

'I think I would have preferred John F Kennedy as a comparison,' he said, 'but if it's this Christie fella you choose, then so be it.'

'I've got a few more questions,' said West. 'Are you ready?'

'Aye, no bother. Fire away.'

'The number plates on the ambulance you drove to and from the robberies, they came off a Corsa in your yard, right?'

'Aye, that's right.'

'Have you switched many number plates before?'

'I'm ashamed to say I have. Not many, but some.'

'And they'd all come off some cars you had lined up for scrap?'

'Correct.'

'And the cars you put them on, I'm guessing they were stolen vehicles, is that right, too?'

'To be honest,' said Keane, 'I couldn't say for sure. I never asked where the vehicles came from but, aye, you'd have to be stupid to think anyone coming to me was selling their car legitimately.'

'What about the people flogging these cars, were they pros? I mean, were they nicking them to order?'

'Hardly,' said Keane. 'Nine out of ten times they were just neds who were after some spare cash. Sometimes they'd walk away with a hundred quid for a car worth five grand.'

'So despite the fact you knew they were stolen, you bought them anyway? And you ringed them?'

'Aye.'

'Did you deal with anyone on a regular basis?'

'One fella,' said Keane. 'I'd not say he was regular, not like a bus or a train, but he'd turn up every now and then.'

'Do you have a name?'

'Rab. Robert.'

'Robert Hines?'

'Aye, that's the lad.'

'How well do you know him?' said West. 'Is he a mate or just an acquaintance?'

'I hardly knew him at all. He'd show up, we'd exchange a few words and share a joke, apart from that all we did was swap keys for cash.'

'When was the last time you saw him?' said West. 'Was it recently?'

Keane slowly lowered his head, coughed, and cradled the cup in both hands.

'What's up?' said West. 'If you've got something to say, Mr Keane, it's probably best to get it out in the open now. It might be worse if you leave it for later.'

'It was a few nights ago,' said Keane. 'I can't remember exactly.'

'Nights? I know you lot like to carry out your business under cover of darkness but isn't that a bit odd?'

'Aye, it was,' said Keane as he gulped his coffee. 'It was very odd indeed.'

'Go on.'

'It was late.'

'How late?'

'Past midnight. He was in a state.'

'How do you mean?'

'Shaken up. Worried.'

'Did he come to you?'

'Aye.'

'Your home or the yard?'

'The yard,' said Keane. 'He was after a lift.'

'Where to?'

'Moffat. He said it was urgent. He said he'd some bits to drop off for the fellas he was working with.'

'And where exactly in Moffat was this?'

'Raehills Meadows,' said Keane. 'He said they were building a rig for a music festival and he had some parts for the lights.'

'What kind of parts?'

'No idea,' said Keane, 'but I remember thinking they couldn't be that important, I mean, it was only a wee package, one of those padded envelopes.'

'So,' said West, 'you gave him a lift. Then what?'

'We got to Raehills, he left the car, and he disappeared behind a stage. A few seconds later, he popped up again but the strange thing was…' Keane paused and wiped his forehead with the cuff of his coat. 'The strange thing was, another fella came along. He was running. He ran across the field towards him.'

'And then?'

'I could hear them arguing, shouting at each other, then it turned into a brawl.'

'Was it serious?'

'I don't know,' said Keane, 'I'm not one for trouble. I didn't want to get involved. I jumped in my car and left them to it.'

'I can't say I blame you,' said West. 'What about Hines, how did he get home?'

'I don't know, and I don't care. I thought, he's a grown man, the town centre's not far away, he could walk and get a cab.'

'Think back,' said West. 'This other bloke, do you remember what he looked like? What he was wearing?'

'Neither,' said Keane. 'Sorry, it was too dark.'

'Any idea where he came from?'

'Not the big house, that was in the other direction. I'm pretty sure he came the same way as us, up the approach road that leads to the meadows.'

'What makes you so sure?'

'I passed a car on the way out,' said Keane. 'It wasn't there before and it was half blocking the road.'

'Can you describe the car?'

'Aye, no problem. Cars, that's what I do. I recognised it straight away. It was a Subaru. Blue. Not in good condition but still worth a few quid.'

West stood, made for the door, and paused.

'Tell me something,' she said. 'Why didn't you mention any of this before?'

'Why should I?' said Keane. 'It's nothing to do with the robberies. Just a couple of neds having a squabble.'

'Fair point,' said West. 'Fair point. Right, I think that's it for now, Mr Keane. If I need another word, I'll try and catch you before you go.'

Chapter 22

Unlike Dougal, whose retentive mind was tailor-made for sitting exams, completing crosswords, and trouncing contestants' lacklustre performances on TV quiz shows, Duncan – who struggled to memorise a shopping list let alone the intricacies of the law – had nonetheless managed to work his way up the ranks driven by a stubborn determination to succeed and a reliance on his prowess at thinking like a criminal, his only failing being a tendency to put too much faith in human nature.

Buoyed by the haul of illicit substances seized from Miller's flat, he returned to the office, dumped the sack on the table, and smiled at Dougal.

'I need a brew,' he said. 'Where's Westy?'

'She's still with Keane.'

'Did you take care of Miller?'

'Aye, he's booked in,' said Dougal, 'and judging by the look on his face I reckon he'll be spending most of his stay sitting on the toilet.'

'Serves him right,' said Duncan. 'I gave that fella inch after inch and all he did was hold out for a mile.'

'What's in the bag?'

'This,' said Duncan, as he opened the sack, 'is Miller's downfall. Exhibit A, cash; and exhibit B, cocaine. Can you get it up to Glasgow for me please, pal. We need to know if it's the same grade as the stuff we found in Freya Thomson's handbag.'

'No bother,' said Dougal, 'but Kay's on her way over, I'll give it to her to sort out.'

* * *

Like a lady of leisure who'd just returned from a relaxing massage and a lengthy spell in a bubbling hot tub, West, looking as pleased as punch, sauntered into the office and pulled up a chair.

'Well, that was a doddle,' she said. 'I think Stuart Keane has to be the most co-operative suspect I've ever had the pleasure of dealing with.'

'I wish the same could be said for wee Jonnie Miller,' said Duncan. 'He's as obstinate as a mule.'

'I thought you had a soft spot for him.'

'Correction,' said Duncan, 'I've a soft spot for folk who deserve a break, folk who have certain difficulties.'

'Well, doesn't Miller fit the bill?'

'Not anymore. I know the fella's not that great when it comes to reading or writing but he's not stupid. He's been taking advantage and it's time he had a wake-up call.'

West looked at the tin of shortbread on the table and smiled.

'Lovely,' she said. 'Do you mind if I…'

'They're not biscuits,' said Duncan, 'it's full of cash, and that there is bag of coke.'

'From Miller's place?'

'Aye. All this time he's sworn blind that the hardest gear he's ever peddled is grass, and then I find this. As far as I'm concerned, the game's a bogey.'

'Good luck with that,' said Dougal. 'If he gets done for possession, he'll probably walk away with a warning.'

'He'll not be walking anywhere,' said Duncan. 'I'm doing him for intent to supply, and theft as well.'

'Have you interviewed him yet?' said West.

'No, I'm about to do it now.'

'Well, sit down for a minute. I've got some ammo for you.'

Still hankering after a mug of tea, Duncan reluctantly perched on the edge of the desk and looked at West.

'I hope it's a missile,' said Duncan, 'and not rubber bullets.'

'It's a missile alright. It's a blooming great Trident. Stuart Keane and Robert Hines were in cahoots with each other. Hines was nicking motors and Keane was ringing them.'

'So the Chief was right, after all?'

'Yup, as usual. Anyway, the same night Freya Thomson was topped, Hines pitched up at Keane's place begging for a lift to Raehills.'

'Are you joking me? And this was *after* Thomson had been killed?'

'Apparently,' said West, 'it was well past midnight. The bottom line is Keane gave him a lift and when they got there, Hines disappeared behind a stage, I'm guessing it's the same one where they found his gear, and when he reappeared some other bloke popped up out of the blue, tore across the field, and started laying into him.'

'You mean verbally?' said Duncan. 'Or was it a fight?'

'Proper fisticuffs by all accounts.'

'And did Keane break it up?'

'No chance,' said West. 'The man's a lightweight. He jumped in his car and legged it.'

'Was he able to identify this other fella?'

'No. Too dark. But get this. On the way out he passed a motor parked on the lane that wasn't there before. It was a blue Subaru.'

'That's what Miller drives.'

'Exactly.'

Duncan held his chin in his hand and scratched the bristles on his cheek.

'So, you're thinking it was Miller tussling with Hines?' he said.

'Yes.'

'And you're thinking it was Miller who *killed* Hines?'

'Double yes! Think about it,' said West. 'We now know Miller was dealing coke. We know Thomson was carrying coke in her handbag, and we know Hines killed Thomson. Join the dots! If the coke belonged to Miller and his motor was spotted at Raehills the night Hines was killed, then it's a done deal!'

Duncan stood and made his way to the door.

'I'm not convinced,' he said. 'Miller may be a lot of things, miss. He's a thief, a fraudster, and a dealer. But he's not a killer.'

* * *

With his straw hat resting on the back of his head like some fly-by-night flogging knock-off sunglasses and sticks of rock to gullible tourists on the pier at Dunoon, Jonnie Miller – feeling chilly in his short-sleeved Fred Perry – rubbed his arms and looked sheepishly at Duncan as he swaggered into the room, sat down, and glared across the table.

'I'm through playing the social worker with you,' he said softly. 'So here's the deal. You can either carry on acting like the selfish, self-centred fool you are and go down for everything I'm about to throw at you, or you can co-operate and I'll see what I can do about getting you a suspended. What's it to be?'

Miller thrust his hands between his knees and forced a smile.

'I'll do my best.'

'You'd better had,' said Duncan, 'because I've got your cash, and I've got your drugs. That adds up to a spell in the big house with the wee windaes.'

Smarting from the mention of his cocaine, Miller took a deep breath, puffed out his cheeks, and heaved a protracted sigh.

'If you put it like that,' he said, 'it looks like I've got no choice.'

Duncan reached across the table and pressed the voice recorder.

'The time is 12:32pm. I'm Detective Sergeant Reid. Please state your full name.'

'Jonnie. Jonathan Miller.'

'Do you understand why you're here, Mr Miller?'

'I do, aye.'

'Good. This morning we seized a haul of Class A drugs and a substantial amount of cash from your flat on Smith Street. Do you admit to possessing said drugs?'

'Aye.'

'Do you admit that the drug mentioned is cocaine?'

'It is, aye.'

'And do you admit that the cash constitutes the proceeds from the sale of said drug?'

'Aye.'

'Excellent,' said Duncan. 'And how long have you been in the business of supplying Class A drugs?'

Miller glanced at Duncan and shrugged his shoulders.

'I'm not sure,' he said. 'A year. Maybe a wee bit less.'

'And where do you get it from?'

Miller hesitated before answering.

'No comment.'

Duncan glowered at Miller and slowly stood.

'I'm disappointed,' he said. 'We were off to such a cracking start. Interview suspended. The time is…'

'Oh, come on!' said Miller. 'If I told you where I got it from, life wouldn't be worth living! They'd do me! Even if you locked me up, they'd still do me!'

'Let's move on,' said Duncan. 'Your dealing. You didn't work alone, did you? You had help. Help in the form of Miss Freya Thomson. Is that correct?'

'It is.'

'And what was Freya's role, exactly?'

'She kept hold of the snow,' said Miller. 'It was safer that way. I'd take orders from the punters then she'd give me the gear I needed.'

Duncan, looking as bored as a patient in a waiting room, leaned against the door and slipped his hands into his pockets.

'Was Freya carrying your drugs during your gig at The Bonnie Selkie?'

'She was,' said Miller. 'Quite a bit, as it happens.'

'How so?'

'We were expecting a big crowd. We weren't disappointed.'

'And what was more upsetting?' said Duncan. 'The fact that Freya was murdered, or the fact that someone had stolen your coke?'

'That's not funny.'

'Damned right, pal. It's not funny at all. It's a tragedy. Your friend, Robert Hines, was he at your gig?'

'Aye. He was.'

'How did you know it was him who'd nicked your gear?'

Miller, taken aback for a second time, stared at Duncan with a look of surprise.

'So, you know it was him, too?'

'I know everything, Jonnie. I'm waiting for an answer.'

'He knew I was dealing,' said Miller. 'He'd bought some gear off me before, but that night he was acting strange. He was watching me like a hawk. All night. Every time I left my deck to go to the bar, I could feel his eyes following me around the room.'

'So, he'd sussed that Freya was carrying your supply?'

'He must have done, aye.'

'So, if you know it was Hines who nicked your coke, then you must also know it was Hines who killed Freya.'

'I guessed as much.'

Duncan looked to the floor and frowned as he scratched the back of his head.

'See here, Jonnie,' he said, quietly, 'now I'm confused. How could you possibly know that Hines had nicked your coke? How could you possibly know, at that point in the evening, that Hines had nicked your coke, unless you already knew that he'd murdered Freya Thomson?'

Miller, looking utterly distraught, squirmed in his seat as his eyes welled with tears.

'I found her,' he said. 'I found her in the toilet.'

'Ho! Back up, pal! What do you mean, you found her?'

'I went looking for her once we'd wound up. I thought she'd be wanting a lift.'

'And this was before Tam McDonnell came back?'

'Aye. Like I say, I found her in the toilet and that's when I noticed her bag was gone.'

Duncan returned to his seat and, refraining from raising his voice, locked eyes with Miller.

'Let's get this straight,' he said. 'You found Freya Thomson bleeding to death in the toilets, and you didn't think to call an ambulance?'

'No.'

'You found a dead girl on the floor and you didn't think to call the police?'

'No.'

'You found the love of your life with a corkscrew in her neck and instead of calling for help, you taped an "out of order" sign on the door and went looking for your drugs?'

'Aye.'

'You're some piece of work, Jonnie Miller. I'll give you that. You're some piece of work.'

Disappointed and mystified that anyone bar a contract killer could be capable of such a callous act, Duncan stood, walked slowly to the end of the room, and paused as he gathered his thoughts.

'Raehills Meadows,' he said. 'How did you know Hines would go to Raehills Meadows?'

'It was a hunch,' said Miller. 'I knew he shared a flat with folk who'd steal his food from the fridge so there was no way he could keep anything secret there. He was working at Raehills. It's outdoors, there's plenty of hiding places, and there's no security. So I took a chance.'

'So you drove there? In your Subaru?'

'Aye.'

'And you found him? And you had a fight?'

'I'd not call it a fight,' said Miller. 'A wee bit of pushing and shoving, that was it.'

'But you didn't get your gear back?'

'No,' said Miller. 'I did not. He threatened me and I'm not a big fella so I backed down.'

'How did he threaten you?'

'He said he'd break my fingers so I couldn't work again.'

'And what happened next?'

'Nothing. I walked away. I went home.'

'And what about Hines?' said Duncan. 'Did he leave at the same time as you?'

'No. I left him sitting on the stage gloating like a school bully.'

'Did you see anyone else while you were there? Anyone at all?'

'Not a soul,' said Miller.

'How so? Was it too dark?'

'It wasn't dark at all. The moon was like a light bulb. You could see everything as clear as day.'

Duncan leaned back and folded his arms.

'Tell me something,' he said, 'do you realise that everything you've done is wrong?'

'Aye, but it's not serious, is it?' said Miller. 'I mean, I've not hurt anyone.'

'You don't think stealing money or leaving Freya for dead in a public toilet is serious?'

'Aye, okay, maybe it is, but it's not murder, is it?'

Of the opinion that some folk through no fault of their own wallowed in blissful ignorance of the law and the subsequent severity of their actions, Duncan, chastising himself for empathising with Miller's errant ways, reluctantly pressed ahead.

'I'm about to charge you,' he said, 'but before I do I must caution you that you do not need to say anything in answer to the charge but anything you do say will be noted and may be used in evidence. Do you understand?'

Miller glanced at Duncan and nodded as he smiled.

'Aye.'

'Jonathan Miller, I'm charging you with the theft of approximately fifteen hundred pounds from the premises known as The Bonnie Selkie on Alloway Street. Do you understand?'

'Aye.'

'I am also charging you under the Misuse of Drugs Act with possession of a Class A substance, and intent to supply. Do you understand?'

'Aye.'

'Do you have anything to say in response to the charges?'

'No.'

'Get yourself some rest, Jonnie. You're going to need it.'

* * *

Like a judge who'd knowingly sentenced an innocent man to hang from the gallows, Duncan, feeling a pang of sympathy for Jonnie Miller, retuned to the office, swept Murdo to his lap, and petted him like a therapy dog.

'I'm shattered,' he said. 'Pure shattered. And I could murder a pint.'

'You've earned it,' said West. 'How'd it go?'

'I've charged him with possession, intent to supply, and theft.'

'I'm surprised you didn't throw attempting to pervert the course of justice, at him, too.'

'It crossed my mind,' said Duncan, 'but he's not actually done anything that would make it stick. Even though he found Freya Thomson's body, he was under no obligation to tell the police about it.'

'Hold on!' said West. 'Are you serious? Are you saying he knew she'd been murdered before Tam McDonnell reported it?'

'That's exactly what I'm saying,' said Duncan. 'Sick as it sounds, he's actually done nothing wrong. At least one thing's for sure. We know it wasn't him who killed Robert Hines.'

Rankled by the ensuing silence, Duncan glanced at a smiling West, then Dougal and Munro, and frowned.

'What's going on?' he said. 'Why are you lot grinning like a bunch of dafties?'

'It's all about instinct,' said Munro. 'And you have it in spades.'

'No offence, Chief, but you're havering like a duffer in a care home. Kay, why are you still here? Dougal said you were going to take care of that coke for me.'

'I will,' said Grogan. 'All in good time. I thought you might like to see these before I go.'

Grogan produced a clear, sealed pouch and slid it across the desk towards him.

'I recovered these from the breaker's yard,' she said. 'Two knives. They're the same style as the one used to kill Robert Hines.'

'Hawkbills?'

'Aye, they're knackered,' said Grogan, 'rusty and as blunt as a butter knife, but the same style, all the same.'

'Well, that's something,' said Duncan, 'but they're circumstantial, they'll not get us anywhere.'

'No. But these might.'

Grogan produced a second bag containing a pair of orange gloves with yellow cuffs and crimson-tipped fingers, held it aloft, and smiled.

'I need to get them analysed,' she said, 'but I bet you anything you like the blood on the fingers belongs to Hines.'

'Do they belong to Stuart Keane?'

'I can't see anyone else wearing them,' said Grogan. 'They were in the ambulance, under the driver's seat and there was a smidge of blood on the door handle, too. I'll do a DNA on the bloods and I'll do the insides of the gloves as well. I'm pretty sure I can find something that's come off Keane.'

'That,' said Duncan, 'is a cracking result.'

'Dougal's offered to do the report for the fiscal,' said West, 'so you can get yourself off. Go have that pint.'

'Roger that, miss.'

'Jimbo, I've got one more thing to do. You go on ahead and get the grub. I'll see you in an hour.'

Chapter 23

Convinced that the evidence they'd gathered was enough to secure a conviction, West – too impatient to wait for written confirmation that the bloods and DNA were a positive match for Robert Hines – bounded into the interview room with a brown, paper sack under her arm and began knotting the strands in Duncan's bowl of spaghetti.

'I told you I'd be back,' she said, beaming. 'How are you feeling?'

'No change since the last time we met,' said Keane. 'I'm fine.'

'Good. Tell me something, Mr Keane, do you watch much telly?'

'Aye, of an evening. Isn't that what most folk do?'

'What do you like most? Is it documentaries? Or comedies? Or soap operas?'

'Anything that's on really.'

'I like those crime dramas,' said West, 'those clever foreign ones where you can never guess the ending. I like the way they keep you hanging on right to the very last episode.'

'I've seen a few of them,' said Keane. 'Not my cup of tea. They're not very true to life.'

'That's where you're wrong,' said West, 'they're much true to life. Especially the twists at the end. It's a bit like you and me.'

'How so?'

'Well, I'm the detective banging her head against the wall trying to solve a particular crime, and you're the suspect who tells me everything I need to know.'

'Is that a compliment?'

'It would be,' said West, 'if your co-operation wasn't just a diversion tactic.'

'I'm not with you.'

West reached for the voice recorder and smiled.

'I'm Detective Inspector West,' she said. 'Would you state your name, please.'

'Again?'

'Name.'

'Stuart Keane.'

'During our last interview you said you gave Robert Hines a lift to Raehills Meadows but you also said you left when another bloke turned up and the two of them started to fight. That's right, isn't it?'

'Aye. Spot on.'

'But it's not true, is it?'

'Of course it is,' said Keane. 'I told you before, I'm not one for trouble, Inspector.'

'Well,' said West, chancing her arm, 'we've got a witness who says otherwise.'

Keane narrowed his eyes, thought for a moment, and smiled.

'I think I know who that is,' he said. 'Would it be the fella in the Subaru?'

'Bang on!' said West. 'Well done, that's exactly who it is. But here's the thing, Mr Keane, you didn't clock that Subaru on your way *out*, did you? You passed it on your way *in*, it was already there. And when Hines and this other bloke started having a barney, you didn't leave, did you? You went back to your car and waited for things to die down.'

Keane, his composure crumbling, blinked and swallowed hard.

'No, no,' he said, defiantly. 'I definitely left. I got in my car and left.'

'For the benefit of the tape,' said West as she reached into the paper sack, 'I am now showing Mr Keane two knives known as hawkbill knives due the shape of the blade. Do you recognise these, Mr Keane?'

Keane leaned forward and scrutinised the knives.

'Aye, they look familiar,' he said. 'Where did you find them?'

'They were in your yard,' said West. 'Obviously they've seen better days but what I'd like to know is, do you use this style of knife a lot?'

'I use many knives,' said Keane, 'but those are particularly good for rope and cables. Why?'

'Because we found one just like these at Raehills Meadows.'

'Well, that's quite a coincidence. Quite a coincidence, indeed.'

'Isn't it just. We also found these,' said West. 'For the benefit of the tape I am now showing Mr Keane a pair of gloves. Are these the kind of gloves you wear, Mr Keane?'

'I've a few pairs similar, aye. They're cheap and cheerful but they do the job. Did you find those at the Meadows, too?'

'I'm afraid not,' said West. 'We found them beneath the front seat of your dodgy ambulance. Look at the fingertips. They've got blood on them. We also found traces of blood on the driver's-side door handle so I suggest you start talking, Mr Keane, or the only way you'll be leaving prison is in a box.'

Keane, biting his bottom lip, stared at West and breathed deeply.

'It's not all lies,' he said as his shoulders sagged. 'I was telling the truth. I did give Hines a lift. And there was a scuffle, but you're right. I didn't leave. I took myself off and kept my head down.'

'And then?'

'I asked Hines what all the hoo-ha was about. He said the fella was after his gear. I said, "*Gear*? What do you mean, *gear*?" Then he explained. He said it was cocaine.'

'Did that shock you?'

'Aye, it did,' said Keane. 'Stealing a car's one thing, but drug-running, that's something else altogether.'

'So what happened next?'

'He told me not to worry. He said, "Just pretend I never mentioned it and you'll be alright."'

'Did you take that as a threat?'

'No, I don't think so, but I said it seemed like a lot of effort for the other fella to go, I mean, driving all the way down to Raehills in the middle of the night. I said he must've thought it was worth it.'

'And what did Hines say?'

'He laughed,' said Keane. 'He said it was worth it. He said the drugs were worth a few thousand pounds.'

'And what did you think of that?'

'I was surprised. I'm not across drugs or dealing or anything like that. I just thought, that's an awful lot of cash to suck up your nose.'

'But that wasn't the end of it, was it?' said West. 'That's when you had your light-bulb moment.'

'I was curious,' said Keane. 'I said how on earth does anyone go about selling thousands of pounds' worth of drugs. He said it was easy. He said once someone knows you've got it, the rest come running.'

'So you thought you'd have a go yourself?'

Keane hung his head and sighed.

'Aye. I did. I was stupid.'

'So what did you do?'

'I pulled my knife.'

'On someone like Hines? You're right, that was stupid.'

'He might be younger than me,' said Keane, 'and a wee bit bigger, but he's not any stronger.'

'So you threatened him with the knife thinking he'd hand the drugs over?'

'Aye.'

'And how did he react?'

'He laughed. Again. It riled me so I jabbed at him but...'

'But what?'

'He grabbed my arm and we spun around. There was a bit of a skirmish and he was under me. The next thing I knew he dropped to the ground.'

'I bet that gave you a fright.'

'Right enough,' said Keane. 'I thought that would make him even more angry so I didn't bother looking for the drugs. I thought when he gets up he'll come after me so I didn't hang around. I left as quick as I could.'

'So a man's dead all because you thought you could make yourself a few quid.'

'Dead?'

'Yup. Robert Hines died of his injury. He died because you killed him.'

Keane threw his head back, covered his face with his hands, and groaned.

'I never knew,' he said. 'Jesus Christ, honest to God, you have to believe me, I never knew.'

'One thing I don't get,' said West, 'is why? If you had this scam going with Ian Barrie. If you were due for a cut from the robberies, you'd have been quids in. So what on earth possessed you to try your hand at dealing?'

'I've no idea,' said Keane. 'Boredom? Boredom and greed? Maybe I was too obsessed about buying a house. Maybe I was too obsessed about giving up the scrap business. Maybe I just wanted a quiet life with Jennie.'

West leaned back and crossed her arms.

'The irony of it is,' she said, 'if you'd played by the rules from the off instead of coming up with these "get rich quick" schemes, you'd have had that house by now. Still, I admire your honesty, Mr Keane. If you're lucky, you might get away with manslaughter, but either way I wouldn't pack your sunglasses if I were you. You won't be seeing daylight for a while.'

Epilogue

As a fiercely independent if not belligerent and sometimes cantankerous widower of five years, James Munro – whose mantra was "buy fresh, buy local" – had, since the passing of his beloved wife, largely avoided the temptation of ready meals and the allure of takeaways, choosing instead to dine on food which was neither frozen nor mass-produced but crafted by hand in the confines of his kitchen.

However, whilst willing to avail himself of the hospitality of friends, his seldom seen ability as a chef was a light he chose to hide in the shade of a bushel.

Alerted to West's imminent arrival by Murdo's frantic scramble for the door, he checked on the oven and reached for the glasses as she strolled into the room.

'Blimey,' she said, 'something smells flipping gorgeous, what are we having?'

'Meatloaf,' said Munro, 'stuffed with Kintyre cheddar and wrapped in Ayrshire bacon.'

'You made it?'

'I most certainly did.'

'Well if I'd known I had Marco Pierre White kipping in the spare room I'd have charged you rent. What's on the side?' said West. 'Broccoli? Peas? Carrots?'

Munro opened the wine and regarded West with a look of disdain.

'If it's greens you're after, there's a hedge outside. We're having mashed tatties, take it or leave it.'

'I'll take all you've got. This is a right treat. The only time anyone ever cooks for me is when you come to stay.'

'Then perhaps you should find yourself a suitor,' said Munro. 'From what I've read, husbands appear to be the latest trend in kitchen gadgets.'

'Don't even go there, Jimbo. Just pour the wine and keep cooking.'

West tossed her jacket on the couch and raised her glass as Munro set the table.

'Cheers,' she said.

'Your very good health. So, have you cleared the decks, Charlie? I'm assuming your "one last thing" in the office was an interview with that Mr Keane?'

'Yup, and I got a right result, too. Apart from his role in the robberies, he's also admitted to killing Robert Hines.'

'Nae need for a polygraph, then.'

'Well, I say kill, he didn't actually know he'd killed him. He stabbed him and legged it.'

'So there was nae intent?'

'None, so he's been charged with culpable homicide.'

'I'm surprised,' said Munro. 'Based on my limited knowledge of the case I was under the impression that Mr Keane was more flight than fight.'

'You, of all people,' said West, 'should know better. It's always the quiet ones. Anyway, how did you guess it was him?'

'I didnae guess, Charlie. I simply defined a possible link between him and Robert Hines. Call it instinct, if you like.'

'Call it what you want,' said West, 'but sometimes that sixth sense of yours is a bit creepy.'

'What's creepy,' said Munro, 'is the way someone like Keane can suddenly turn violent. Did he not give you a reason for his actions? A reason for going after the cocaine?'

'He did, but it's nothing exciting. He claims it was boredom, or greed, or maybe just a mid-life crisis. Either way, none of this would have happened if he wasn't such a lazy bugger.'

'How so?'

'He's spent his entire life looking for the easy way out. A scam here, a fiddle there. If he'd followed the rules and paid his taxes from the off, he wouldn't be in the mess he's in now.'

'Right enough,' said Munro. 'Him and half the population.'

Munro pulled the sizzling meatloaf from the oven, sliced it in two, and placed it on the table alongside a bowl of buttery mashed potatoes.

'Voilà,' he said, as he took a seat. 'Pain de viande écossaise avec pomme purée. Bon appétit.'

'I was wrong,' said West. 'It's not Marco Pierre White in the spare room, it's blooming Albert Roux.'

'It's fine dining, lassie, and it comes with a price, of course.'

'I knew it,' said West, 'there's always a caveat with you. Come on then, what's the catch?'

'Dishes. You can do the dishes.'

'Great. I bet Duncan doesn't have this problem when he gets home. I bet his missus cooks his supper, and does the dishes, and makes him a pudding as well.'

'Well, I'm not your missus,' said Munro. 'Besides, I'd say he deserves it, wouldn't you?'

'Too right. He's played a blinder this week.'

'Young Dougal's had his moments, too.'

'Granted, and I'm not denying it, but as far as Duncan's concerned I think I'm going to have to watch my back. There's only room for one DI in the office and I'm staying put. What about you?'

'What about me, Charlie?'

'Are you staying put or are you heading back to Auchencairn?'

'The latter.'

'Please tell me you're not knocking down more walls.'

'No, no,' said Munro. 'The fireplace. In the back room.'

'I thought that was bricked up.'

'It is but wee Murdo's rather curious about something behind it.'

'Gawd, I don't like the sound of that,' said West. 'I hope it's just a flipping pigeon.'

'It could be a missing person,' said Munro. 'There's a couple of cold cases in the area.'

'I'm rapidly going off the idea of moving there, you know that, don't you?'

'Och, away, lassie! You'll enjoy it. In fact you should join me, bring your overalls and muck in. After all, it's you who's going to be living there, you may as well make your mark on the place.'

'That's not a bad idea,' said West. 'Alright, you're on. In fact I've just bought some curtains, if you put a rail up we could hang them.'

'That's settled then. You'll not regret it.'

West pushed her plate to one side, took a sip of wine, and gazed wistfully into space.

'Actually,' she said, 'now I think about it, I can't wait. It'll be like one of those mini-breaks. A couple of days in a cosy country cottage.'

'It'll be nothing of the sort,' said Munro. 'It'll be like camping indoors.'

'Oh well, an adventure, then.'

'Not an adventure either,' said Munro. 'More a test of endurance, Charlie. Aye, that's the word. Endurance.'

Character List

JAMES MUNRO (RETIRED) – Despite a desire to single-handedly renovate his newly acquired cottage, the indefatigable James Munro is distracted by news of an unexplained death outside of his jurisdiction as a volunteer with the Ayrshire force and consequently causes ructions in neighbouring Dumfries and Galloway as he endeavours to solve the case guided by instinct rather than facts.

DI CHARLOTTE WEST – With a vicious murder, a theft, a drug dealer, and a string of armed robberies to deal with, the capricious "Charlie" West, as unpredictable as the weather, relies on the support of her team as she balances leadership with a grassroots investigation.

DS DOUGAL McCRAE – Utilising his skills as a technology expert with an eye for detail, the bookish DS McCrae is forced to relinquish his predilection for working at night as he unearths a convoluted plot to steal luxury items from a handful of high-end retailers.

DS DUNCAN REID – Cut from the same cloth as the sagacious DI Munro, the maverick DS Reid, whose respect for the rule book is often in doubt, is given the run-around by a key witness as he works tirelessly to track down a drug dealer suspected of murder.

DCI GEORGE ELLIOT – The ebullient DCI Elliot, suffering from weight loss as a result of his wife's desire to share her bed with a slimmer man, embraces Munro's company at the dinner table and his timely, though unauthorised involvement in a case.

DR ANDY McLEOD – Forensic pathologist Andy McLeod, accepting that in the absence of a date with DI West, he was destined to remain single, discovers a link between two seemingly unconnected cases.

KAY GROGAN – The enthusiastic scenes of crime officer with a passion for forensics, microfibres, blood, and skin, gathers invaluable evidence from a series of incidents and offers her own unqualified but welcome view on exactly what happened.

TAM McDONNELL – A retired advertising executive relocates from the east coast to open a bar in the hope of spending his twilight years pulling pints and havering over a dram until the death of a customer almost forces him shut up shop.

JONNIE MILLER – Part-time DJ and full-time racketeer, the young Jonnie Miller is always on the lookout for pies needing a finger but his greed and cocky self-assurance soon conspire to create his downfall.

FREYA THOMSON – As pure as the driven snow, the petite Freya Thomson, a self-employed barmaid possessed with a talent for cajoling customers into buying more than they wanted, hides behind a veil of contentment to disguise the heartbreak of the past.

CHARLES BEWLEY – A connoisseur of the finer things in life, the aging Bewley, whose unassailable knowledge of whisky keeps him at the top of his game, succumbs to the allure of a much younger lady and lives to regret it.

MORAG FLEMING – Housekeeper, confidante, and cook to Charles Bewley, the libidinous Fleming, a victim of unrequited love, tries her hand at seducing the younger generation.

DI GREG BYRNE – Finally accepting his responsibilities as a DI and covering his own ineptitude by delegating everything he can, the incompetent DI Byrne welcomes Munro's involvement as a way of offloading a case.

DC DANIEL CLARK – A young detective more concerned with his image and the pulling power of his badge gets short shrift from a senior officer when interrogated over the death of a labourer.

HANNAH COX – As a self-employed courier with a passion for driving, the young Hannah Cox, living life to the full, has her world turned upside down when her friend and flatmate is unexpectedly murdered.

SOPHIE TAYLOR – An experienced hand in the art of hospitality, Sophie Taylor, a fixture at the Ayr Racecourse Hotel for several years, is shocked by the news of her flatmate's death.

NEIL IRVINE – At the helm of a fourth-generation jewellery business, Neil Irvine, not ashamed to flaunt his family wealth, falls victim to a couple of chancers intent on relieving him of his trinkets.

SCOTT McCALLUM – Assistant to Neil Irvine, the fresh-faced McCallum's only real talent is his ability to smile and process payments from customers with more money than sense.

STUART KEANE – As a scrap metal merchant and the owner of a breaker's yard, the middle-aged Keane has spent his entire life earning a living on the wrong side of the law and suddenly comes unstuck when, unable to provide any proof of his earnings, he is denied a mortgage and looks for other ways to boost his income.

JENNIE FERGUSON – Common law wife to Stuart Keane, Jennie is content doing nothing more than running the house and keeping bailiffs from the door until the opportunity to gain a little acting experience ignites something in her soul.

IAN BARRIE – As a high-rolling doctor on a locum's salary, Ian Barrie had the means to do as he pleases, when he pleases, with whomever he pleases, until an unforced error leads to an inquiry about his professional conduct.

If you enjoyed this book, please let others know by leaving a quick review on Amazon. Also, if you spot anything untoward in the paperback, get in touch. We strive for the best quality and appreciate reader feedback.

editor@thebookfolks.com

www.thebookfolks.com

ALSO BY PETE BRASSETT

In this series:

SHE – book 1
AVARICE – book 2
ENMITY – book 3
DUPLICITY – book 4
TERMINUS – book 5
TALION – book 6
PERDITION – book 7
RANCOUR – book 8
PENITENT – book 9
TURPITUDE – book 10
HUBRIS – book 11
PENURY – book 12

Other titles:

THE WILDER SIDE OF CHAOS
YELLOW MAN
CLAM CHOWDER AT LAFAYETTE AND SPRING
THE GIRL FROM KILKENNY
BROWN BREAD
PRAYER FOR THE DYING
KISS THE GIRLS

SHE

With a serial killer on their hands, Scottish detective Munro and rookie sergeant West must act fast to trace a woman observed at the crime scene. Yet discovering her true identity, let alone finding her, proves difficult. Soon they realise the crime is far graver than either of them could have imagined.

AVARICE

A sleepy Scottish town, a murder in a glen. The local police chief doesn't want a fuss and calls in DI Munro to lead the investigation. But Munro is a stickler for procedure, and his sidekick Charlie West has a nose for a cover up. Someone in the town is guilty, will they find out who?

ENMITY

When it comes to frustrating a criminal investigation, this killer has all the moves. A spate of murders is causing havoc in a remote Scottish town. Enter Detective Inspector Munro to catch the red herrings and uncover an elaborate and wicked ruse.

DUPLICITY

When a foreign worker casually admits to the murder of a local businessman, detectives in a small Scottish town guess that the victim's violent death points to a more complex cause. Money appears to be a motive, but will anyone believe that they might be in fact dealing with a crime of passion?

TERMINUS

Avid fans of Scottish detective James Munro will be worrying it is the end of the line for their favourite sleuth when, battered and bruised following a hit and run, the veteran crime-solver can't pin down a likely suspect.

TALION

A boy finds a man's body on a beach. Police quickly suspect foul play when they discover he was part of a local drugs ring. With no shortage of suspects, they have a job pinning anyone down. But when links to a local business are discovered, it seems the detectives may have stumbled upon a much bigger crime than they could have imagined.

PERDITION

A man is found dead in his car. A goat is killed with a crossbow. What connects these events in a rural Scottish backwater? DI Charlotte West investigates in this gripping murder mystery that ends with a sucker punch of a twist.

RANCOUR

When the body of a girl found on a mountainside tests positive for a date rape drug, police suspect a local Lothario is responsible. He certainly had the means, motive and opportunity. But is this really such a cut and dry case? What are the detectives missing?

PENITENT

The shady past of a small town surfaces when a young woman is found murdered in a pool. As detectives investigate, a legacy of regret and resentment emerges. DI Munro and DI West must get to the bottom of the matter.

TURPITUDE

A murdered jeweller, a series of bungled moped robberies and several fingers found at a refuse site. What connects these events? That's what DI Charlie West and her team must find out, with a little bit of help from Munro. But will the latter be too distracted by his new friend to be of much help?

HUBRIS

When a dead sailor is found in a boat, detective Charlie West is tasked with finding out why. But getting answers from a tight-knit Scottish fishing community won't be easy, and besides, has the killer completely covered their tracks?

PENURY

A property developer is found dead after acquiring a hotel. The last person to see her alive is murdered shortly after. DI James Munro assists DI Charlotte West's team and the inexperienced DI Greg Byrne as they unravel a web of lies.

For more great books, visit: www.thebookfolks.com

Made in the USA
Columbia, SC
28 January 2022

54969563R00124